14

D0611312

DEFINITELY DECEASED

DEFINITELY DECEASED

Roderic Jeffries

This first world edition published in Great Britain 2001 by
SEVERN HOUSE PUBLISHERS LTD of
9–15 High Street, Sutton, Surrey SM1 1DF.
This first world edition published in the USA 2001 by
SEVERN HOUSE PUBLISHERS INC. of
595 Madison Avenue, New York, NY 10022.

British Library Cataloguing in Publication Data

Jeffries, Roderic, 1926–
   Definitely deceased. – (An Inspector Alvarez novel)
   1. Alvarez, Inspector (Fictitious character)
   2. Police – Spain
   3. Majorca (Spain)
   4. Detective and mystery stories
   I. Title
   823.9′14 [F]

ISBN 0–7278–5730–4

Typeset by Palimpsest Book Production Limited,
Polmont, Stirlingshire, Scotland.
Printed and bound in Great Britain by
MPG Books Ltd, Bodmin, Cornwall.

One

The sargento brought the car to a halt, but ignored the slight slope they were on with the consequence that he had hastily to apply the handbrake, to the other's silent, sarcastic amusement. He stared through the windscreen. 'What a dump!' He spoke to his junior, a cabo, with the scorn of someone born and brought up in Barcelona.

Where the cabo had lived, there were many farms like this one.

'I reckon this can't be Ca'n Portens.'

'The man we asked back on the road said that this is where Munar lives.'

'By the look of him, he's so simple he'd tell you he lived in a castle.'

'Just a typical countryman wanting to appear a lot less smart than he is.' And by the same token, the cabo thought, townspeople often tried to appear a lot smarter than they were.

'What's that in the left-hand side of the house, for God's sake?'

'A Friesian, from the colouring.'

'A bloody cow! I suppose they bed down with it at night for company?'

'The living quarters will be on the top floor. In the old days, most farms were built that way so the more valuable animals would be secure at night.'

1

'If you ask me, it's a miracle the locals ever moved out of those stone huts.'

'D'you mean the talayots?'

'If that's what they're called.'

'They date back thousands of years.'

'So do the locals.'

'The talayots are Bronze Age. Some of the stones weigh over eight tons and there's doubt how they were hauled around and put in place.'

'How come you know so much about this island?'

'I've a girl friend who lives in Inca.'

'So how d'you get her to understand what you're after?' The sargento sniggered. 'With sign language?' He opened the car door, stepped out on to the hard dirt surface. 'It's like a furnace and it's still only June.' He used a handkerchief to mop his face and neck, replaced it in his grey-green trousers.

The land rose slowly until, well beyond the house, it abruptly became mountainside on which pine trees somehow found sufficient sustenance. The oblong, stone house was uncompromisingly utilitarian in character; the left half of the bottom floor was a barn and the cow, which so offended the sargento, stood in the open doorway as it placidly watched them. Some of the land in front of the house was cultivated, but the condition of the lettuces, peppers, radishes, and beans showed how poor was the soil – even the several olive trees, twisted by centuries, bore the strain of a harsh life. Several sheep, some with lambs to foot, pessimistically searched for food.

'Would someone making a fortune live in a God-forsaken place like this?' the sargento asked.

'The bird with the brightest plumage is the first to get shot.'

'What the hell's that supposed to mean?'

'Where I come from, a man who's making big black money takes care to hide that fact by appearing to be poor.'

'So where do you come from?'

'Begudo.'

'Never heard of it.'

'It's a village not far from Villafranca.'

'No wonder you talk daft.' The sargento looked back at the house. 'I'd have to be hiding a bloody fortune before I'd live in a ruin like this . . . Let's move.'

As they neared the house, a large black dog came through the doorway to the right of the barn, then stopped and stared at them. It began to growl.

'Belt up!' The sargento waved his arms.

'Take it easy. These local dogs can be quite fierce.'

'And I can be a sight fiercer.'

A man appeared, to stand by his dog. Unshaven, hair tangled, dressed in a patched and faded shirt, trousers with a triangular tear at the knee, and scuffed shoes, he would have aroused considerable compassion as a beggar.

'Munar?' the sargento called out.

He considered the question.

The sargento's temper shortened. 'Are you deaf?'

The dog's growls grew louder and it bared its teeth.

'If that cur tries to bite me, I'll shoot it.' The sargento put his right hand down on to the butt of his holstered automatic.

Munar gave an order in Mallorquin and the dog, after one final growl, retired, tail down, into the house.

'It's illegal to keep savage dogs,' the sargento said.

'He ain't savage; only growls when it's necessary.' Munar's Castilian was heavily accented.

'So explain to me now why you reckon it was necessary?'

3

His expression became vacuous.

'Are you, or aren't you Miguel Munar?'

'That's me,' he finally admitted.

'Why didn't you say so when I first asked?'

'Didn't know why you was asking.'

'It's not up to you to know. I ask questions, you answer 'em. D'you understand that?'

He mumbled something.

'Do you expect us to go on standing out in this bloody heat?'

'You want to go inside?'

'Unless you'd prefer us to take you back to the post and keep you there until we can find the time to question you.'

Munar turned and disappeared from sight.

'It's like talking to a dead donkey, isn't it?' the sargento said.

'Can't say, never having tried,' the cabo replied.

'Mark this, Vicente, and mark it goddamn well. If there's one person annoys me more than a stupid cabo, it's a stupid cabo who reckons he's a humorist.'

They entered through the narrow doorway and climbed steep wooden steps that were badly worn. At the top was an oblong room, dimly lit because there was only the one small, glassless window. The floor was bare, rough concrete and the ceiling was the sloping underside of the thin bamboos, between which cement had oozed, that supported the roof tiles; the furniture consisted of two armchairs and a settee of the poorest quality, a traditional table with a brass container underneath in which charcoal was burned for heating, two goatskins used as mats, a framed, religious print, and – the one touch of luxury – a large wide-screen television.

The sargento, determined to mark his authority, did not wait to be invited to sit; he crossed to the nearer armchair and settled heavily. He swore as he hastily tried to find a more comfortable position. 'What the hell's in this seat – nuts and bolts?'

Munar, looking as if he were chewing something, answered: 'It's very old.'

'Came out of the Ark from the feel of it . . . You know why we're here, don't you?'

Munar rubbed his stubbled chin. 'When I took the car for the test, they said there was work needed, but there hasn't been the time to get to the garage . . .'

'You think I'm interested in your poxy car?'

'You ain't?'

'Where were you Wednesday, last week?'

'Wednesday?'

'Isn't that what I've just said?'

'Last week?'

'I'm rapidly losing my temper which means you're very close to spending time in jail.'

'For why?'

'Not answering my questions.'

'What questions?'

The sargento lost his temper and swore in colourful, obscene terms.

The cabo said, speaking without any hint of blustery authority: 'We've an investigation under way and need to know where were you last Wednesday evening?'

Several seconds passed before Munar, still standing, answered. 'I were here, like always.'

'That's a lie!' the sargento snapped. 'You were in Cala Balera. And don't you try saying you don't know what it's used for.'

'Can't rightly say about that. There's no beach, so it ain't for tourists . . .'

'Which is why contraband comes into the cove. You were there last Wednesday, unloading booze and cigarettes.'

'I don't smoke.'

'So that leaves more to sell to the café owners who'll buy 'em because you islanders seem to think you can laugh at the law. But for the likes of you, the laugh's going to be on the other side of the face.'

'Don't understand,' Munar mumbled.

The cabo, again quietly, said: 'You were there when the last load arrived.'

'I were here—'

'Like hell you were!' snapped the sargento.

'—working the land. Only that don't do no good because it's mostly stones and rocks. Even the goats don't grow proper—'

'One of your mates has coughed and told us you were there.'

Momentarily, Munar's expression was one of anger; then it once more became vacuous.

The sargento, who had not missed the reaction, said: 'Your mate has fingered you, so you'll know who to thank for spending years inside . . . Unless you reckon maybe you'd like to talk about it.' He tried to speak with some amiability. 'Co-operate, tell us who else was there, and we'll put in a good word for you. The judges like helpful people and let 'em off lightly. That's really worth it, when every day in a stinking jail is like ten outside.'

Munar might not have heard.

The sargento's manner reverted to aggressive. 'Act dumb and we'll pass word you're an uncooperative bastard. That'll earn you extra time inside.'

'I don't know nothing.'

'Shall I tell you how I'm thinking? What about taking you in now and sweating the truth out of you?'

The cabo, his friendly sympathy in part genuine, said: 'It makes sense to help us. Why suffer more than's necessary?

6

We know you were at Cala Balera last Wednesday evening around twenty thirty hours, so why not admit it? We've been told you was unloading, but maybe the truth is, you was just a look-out. That would help. It ain't the same as actually handling the cargo. And maybe you didn't even know for certain what was coming ashore . . .'

'When the boat came sneaking into the cove and they was keeping a look-out for the law?' said the sargento with angry sarcasm. 'Next thing, you'll be asking if he reckoned the government was going to pay his wages for the night.' He turned to face Munar. 'You were smuggling, so don't waste any more of our time with lying.'

'I was here. Ask the old woman.'

'You think we'd believe your wife?'

'Then ask the foreigner.'

'What foreigner?'

'Him what drove up wanting to know where the other foreigners lived.'

'Who was he?'

'How would I know?'

'And who were the foreigners he was looking for? I don't suppose you know that either!'

'He said, but I don't remember.'

'What a convenient memory!'

'It's the truth.'

'You wouldn't know the truth if it came up and kicked you.'

'It was in the evening when the sun was getting low . . .'

'Not as low as you're going to end up.'

The cabo said: 'Did the foreigner speak Spanish?'

'He tried, but it weren't no good.'

'Then how did you understand what he wanted?'

'He used a book what he got out of the car.'

'A phrase book?'

7

Munar shrugged his shoulders.

'Do you know what nationality he was?'

'English.'

'How can you be certain of that?'

'He showed me what was written in the book. Some was in English, some in Castilian.'

'As if you could read!' The sargento stood. 'I've heard enough crap. You weren't here Wednesday evening, talking to some foreigner, you were in Cala Balera helping to shift a cargo. So until you admit that, we'll be visiting. And mark this, the more times you make us come here, the longer you'll be spending in jail.' He turned, strode across the room, clumped his way downstairs and out.

When the cabo joined him at the car, he said: 'Every time I worked him ready to admit the truth, you started talking soft and gave him time to recover. Are they all as useless as you in Begudo?'

Catalans worked hard to justify their reputation, the cabo thought.

Two

'It's never been this hot before in June,' Jaime said. 'God knows what it'll be like in July and August.' He picked another cube of ice out of the insulated container and dropped it into his drink. 'Too hot for work, that's for sure.'

'For you,' Dolores, Jaime's wife, called from the kitchen, 'even in the middle of winter, it is too hot to do anything but drink.'

He looked uncertainly at the bead curtain which covered the doorway into the kitchen, leaned across and lowered his voice to a murmur. 'How does she know what I'm saying when she's in the kitchen?'

'Women have better hearing than men,' Alvarez, sitting on the other side of the dining-room table, answered.

'Because they can't stand not knowing what a man's talking about.'

'Or not talking about.'

'How's that?'

'Forget it,' Alvarez answered, certain an explanation would have to be a long one and it was too hot for that.

There was a rush of sound and Juan ran into the room. 'Isn't it ready yet?' He faced the bead curtain and shouted: 'How long before grub?'

Dolores put her head between the strings of beads. 'What's that?'

'I'm starving. When's lunch?'

'When I have finished cooking. Have you washed your hands?'

'Sure.'

'Go upstairs and wash them.'

'But I've just said—'

'I heard you.'

'But if it's not time to eat . . .'

'It is time for you to go upstairs and wash.' She withdrew and the strings of plastic beads swung against each other with diminishing force.

Juan stamped his way across to the stairs and up them.

'Typical!' Jaime muttered sourly.

'When you were his age, didn't you object to being told to wash your hands?' Alvarez asked.

'He comes in and shouts and she doesn't hear; I say something real quiet and she's listening to every word.'

'Wish for the sun and it'll rain; wish for rain and it'll be sunny.'

There was a call from the kitchen. 'And let a wife wish her man will lay the table and she'll be even more disappointed.'

Fifteen minutes later, when the family was seated around the table and Dolores was finally serving herself, the phone rang. She emptied another spoonful of Bacalla a la Mallorquina on to her plate. 'Am I the only one who is not deaf?'

'Depends if it's a private conversation . . .' Jaime began and then, for once, heeded discretion and did not finish what he had been going to say.

'The phone is still ringing,' she snapped.

Alvarez swallowed his mouthful. 'It won't be for me at this time of the day.'

'Who would ring me?' Jaime asked through a mouthful.

'I often wonder why the Good Lord gave men legs since the only time they use them is when a drink is not within reach.' She put her plate down on the table, left and made her way through to the front room.

When he heard her talking, Jaime, his tone resentful, spoke to Alvarez. 'Have you noticed how recently she's been on more and more about drinking?'

'Probably because she heard the doctor on the telly saying that wine was only good for one when drunk in moderation.'

'And what did he mean by "moderation"? One glassful a day. Might as well just have water.'

'So d'you want me to pass you the water?' Juan asked, and sniggered.

'Any more stupidity from you and it'll be straight up to your room when you get back from school this afternoon.'

'And make him stay there so as he can't bother Eloísa and me,' Isabel suggested.

'You think I want anything to do with you two?' Juan asked with deep scorn.

'You did when she—'

'Shut up,' Jaime snapped, 'or the two of you will go up to your rooms now.'

Dolores returned and sat. She ate a mouthful. 'Perhaps the cod is a trace too salty and I should have soaked it for longer?'

Alvarez hastened to disagree. 'I wouldn't say that.'

She had another mouthful. 'And a little more garlic would not have hurt.'

'And neither could it have improved perfection.'

'It is absurd to talk like that.' She chided him for his over-fulsome praise while accepting that it was justified.

He hoped he'd massaged her culinary pride sufficiently to ensure peace.

'That was Cousin Luisa who phoned.'

Jaime ignored the need for discretion. As he reached across for the bottle of wine, he said: 'You haven't got a Cousin Luisa.'

'You know more about my family than I do? Or has the wine already taken command of your tongue?'

Drop the subject! Alvarez silently shouted at Jaime.

It was not a good day for telepathy.

'Your uncle didn't have any children and none of your aunts called their daughters Luisa.'

'For me, a relationship is a relationship; perhaps she is a distant cousin, but cousin nevertheless. For you, no doubt, relationships are only found through alcohol.'

'It's not right to talk like that in front of the children.'

'Better they should learn the truth now than at your graveside.'

'Now you're burying me?'

'Did the doctor not say that every drink beyond one a day robs a man of minutes of his future? Since your life expectancy now has a negative value, we must be prepared.'

'He was talking nonsense . . . Enrique, haven't you told me your uncle didn't manage to drink himself to death until he was ninety-six?'

Alvarez did not answer. It was incredible that even after many years of marriage, Jaime still had not learned not to argue with Dolores when she was being irrational. He concentrated on his food, no difficult task since it was almost as delicious as he had earlier suggested. There were those who denigrated dried cod, but when skilfully cooked with onion, flour, white wine (more than a glassful), lemon, garlic, and parsley, it became a noble dish.

'It was Cousin Luisa who phoned,' Dolores said, placing much emphasis on the word 'Cousin'. 'She is very worried, which is why she phoned me.'

'Why bother you when she hasn't seen you in years?' Jaime asked.

'Because she knows I will not reject her merely because it is a long time since I last saw her, unlike someone who will not help his nearest even if he sees her every day.'

'All I'm saying is—'

'There's no need to say anything. Even were you willing to help, there is nothing you can do.'

'If there were, naturally I'd do it.'

'How bravely a man will proclaim himself a warrior when he knows he will not be called upon to fight! . . . I told Cousin Luisa that Enrique would drive over immediately and speak to her.'

'Me?' Alvarez said uneasily.

'She has been worrying so much, she feels ill. I told her, that is stupid and she should have been in touch immediately. What are relations and friends for if not to help?'

'What's her problem?'

'Miguel is being persecuted.'

'Then she should go to the Guardia and lay a complaint.'

'It is the Guardia who are persecuting him.'

'That's ridiculous.'

'Perhaps you would like to hear what happened before you pass an opinion? Time and again, a sargento – a forastero since he is from the Peninsula – arrives at their house and accuses Miguel, no matter how often he swears he knows nothing.'

'Accuses him of what?'

'Smuggling. Miguel tells him, he is only a farmer who tries to make a living working land that is more stone than soil, but the sargento is a Catalan so he refuses to listen and threatens Miguel will soon be in jail. Small wonder that Luisa has become desperate! But I assured her, soon her worries will be forgotten because Enrique will make certain Miguel is no longer persecuted.'

'I can't interfere . . .'

'What do you say?' she demanded, her expression tight, her dark brown eyes filled with challenge.

'I'd really like to be able to do something,' Alvarez answered hurriedly. 'As you said, it's a pleasure to help a relative. But smuggling comes under the Guardia's jurisdiction, so the investigation is entirely in their hands. If I try to interfere, they'll complain to the superior chief and he'll give me hell. It's my duty not to interfere.'

'Let a man start talking about his duty and one can be certain he is trying to evade doing it.'

'It's not evasion, but a question of rules and regulations. And look at things logically. Obviously the Guardia have reason to think Miguel is mixed up with some smuggling—'

'And you wish to use their stupidity as an excuse for doing nothing? You and my husband have much in common!'

'I told you—' Jaime began.

'Then there is no need to repeat nonsense.' She faced Alvarez once more. 'You refuse to help Cousin Luisa?'

There could be a time when a punctilious respect for rules was inadvisable. 'I suppose I could have a word with her as a friend rather than a member of the Cuerpo.'

'You can speak to her immediately after a very brief siesta.'

'I have some work that needs doing . . .'

'It can wait.'

'Try telling Salas that.'

'If necessary.'

She would not have hesitated to tell the superior chief how to run the Cuerpo. 'Where exactly is their place?'

'In Exchau Valley.'

'Oh! I rather thought from the way you were talking that they lived in my area.'

'What does it matter where they do?'

'Exchau Valley lies in Inspector Fuster's area. He's the kind of man who'd refuse to understand I was acting as a friend, not in my authority as a member of the Cuerpo, and would complain to Salas if he ever learned what happened. Then there really would be trouble.'

'Isn't he a member of the Cuerpo?'

'Yes.'

'Did you not say smuggling is the concern of the Guardia, not the Cuerpo? So how can he ever learn you have spoken to Cousin Luisa and Miguel?'

There were times when he wished she was no smarter than her husband. 'In theory, he wouldn't. But things happen differently in practice. The Guardia may well ask Fuster if he knows anything about Miguel and being a man who sticks his nose everywhere it's not wanted, he may get inquisitive and somehow learn I've been talking to Miguel. With his small-minded, mean nature, he'd immediately imagine I was butting into his territory and complain to the superior chief.'

'How easily a man can find reason for doing nothing.'

'If their finca was in my area, I'd forego my siesta and drive there immediately after the meal.'

'If a lie is to be believed, it must be possible to believe it.'

'Why won't you understand that my hands are tied?'

'I understand you have no desire to untie them.'

'That's unfair.'

She turned to Isabel. 'Remember this. When a man claims you are being unfair, you can know he has dredged up sufficient self-respect to be ashamed of himself.'

*   *   *

15

Alvarez reached across the dining-room table for the bottle of brandy. 'It's very quiet in there,' he said, nodding in the direction of the kitchen.

'She's out,' Jaime replied.

'When it's nearly supper time?'

'She was doing some cooking before she left.'

'That's all right, then.' He poured out a generous brandy. 'I've been a bit worried about the way things might go . . . She can become difficult if she doesn't get her own way.'

'You reckon you have to tell me that?'

He drank. 'Maybe she's cooked Greixonera de xot. Remember the last time?'

'Can't say I do.'

'The lamb was as tender as a virgin's kiss.'

Jaime sniggered. 'I'd rather the kiss.'

'When you were in the bedroom for the siesta, did she mention me?'

'Couldn't stop.'

'Maybe she can't understand why I can't do anything to help?'

'Says you never think of anyone but yourself.'

It was always family first and last with her. And, Alvarez acknowledged, he had every cause to be grateful that this was so since she and Jaime provided him with a home. In days when the once strong family ties were breaking down, even to the extent that there were those who were no longer willing to look after their aged parents, such a regard for family values was to be honoured. He must make her realize that he understood this. He would buy her the most expensive selection of chocolates in the shop next to the church. And then she, knowing what he'd spent, would appreciate that his course really was shaped by forces beyond his control. 'What do you know about Luisa and Miguel?'

'Haven't seen 'em in ages; might not even recognize 'em. I've been told her family wasn't keen on the marriage, him being a rough sort, but she was getting on in years and there wasn't no one else interested.'

'Is there a family?'

'Two sons, who both live on the Peninsula and, from what she's said, don't see much of the old people. She says it's the wives are to blame – which makes a difference.'

There was a silence, which Alvarez broke. 'Would you like to do something for me?'

Jaime did not try to sound enthusiastic. 'Depends.'

'When the time seems right, tell Dolores I've said more than once how I wish I could help Luisa and Miguel.'

'You think she'll believe me?'

'If you speak convincingly.'

'The more I try to do that, the more she thinks I'm lying.'

They heard the front door shut. Seconds later, Dolores came into the room, a plastic shopping bag in one hand. She looked hard and long at the bottle on the table, then carried on through to the kitchen.

Jaime drained his glass. 'I don't want any more, thanks,' he said loudly as he reached across for the bottle and then silently poured himself another drink.

A few minutes later, Dolores came through the bead curtain, carrying clean cutlery on a tray. She laid the table, returned into the kitchen without having spoken.

Jaime leaned forward and whispered: 'I can never make up my mind what's worse – her giving me hell or saying nothing and making me wonder what she's thinking.'

'Choose the former. Reality is never as bad as imagination.'

Dolores returned, placed an earthenware pot on a mat on the table, and started serving. She passed a plate to Jaime.

He put it down in front of himself. 'What's this?'

'Cuirons amb sofrit,' she answered with careless indifference.

'You know I don't like 'em,' he said, staring at the chick peas in a tomato and onion sauce.

'It's good for the soul to enjoy something one dislikes.'

'If I dislike 'em, how the hell can I enjoy 'em?'

'By considering your soul rather than your stomach.'

A tall order, Alvarez thought, as he was passed a plate. But really, Jaime was complaining before there was need to. True, chick peas would never make a gourmet meal, but the sauce would be delicious . . . The peas were not cooked and the sauce tasted of cardboard. He wondered if she'd suddenly been taken ill, but a quick glance failed to discern any sign of illness. However, there was a suggestion of satisfaction in her expression. Illness, nothing! The meal was deliberately unappetising. But if she thought she could weaken his resolve in so underhand and typically feminine a way . . .

Lunch on Thursday was cold, sinewy ham, half-cooked boiled potatoes, and stringy beans; pudding was green bananas and stale almonds. And because Dolores had 'forgotten' to buy more red wine, Alvarez and Jaime could only have half a tumbler each.

It was a game at which two could play. As Alvarez stood, he said: 'That was a delicious meal!' He laughed to himself as he walked away. His words would rankle all the time she was cleaning the table; they might even upset her siesta. Women so often overrated their capacity for cunning. He began to climb the stairs.

'By the way,' she said casually, plates in one hand, glasses in the other, 'I'm going out this evening so—'

'You what?' Jaime's voice was high.

She repeated what she'd just said.

'Why?'

'Because I wish to.'

'Where d'you think you're going?'

'I know where I'm going.'

'What I want to know—'

'Is even less than you have the capacity to understand. As I won't be here to cook a meal, I'll leave some sandwiches.'

'What d'you mean, sandwiches?'

'I wasn't able to buy fresh bread this morning, so I'll have to make them from yesterday's.'

Stale bread and stringy ham for supper? What horror was proposed for lunch the next day? . . . Alvarez descended three stairs. He spoke to Dolores. 'You know, I'd really like to do what I can for Miguel, so I'll have a word with him tomorrow and to hell with Inspector Fuster.'

Her expression became one of amused tolerance for men's weaknesses.

Three

When Alvarez left his car and walked towards Ca'n Portens, his emotion was not contempt, as had been the sargento's, but gratitude that there were still parts of the island which had not been overwhelmed by outside forces. Here was honesty, perhaps bleak, but then honesty so often was. The man who struggled with the land and the elements rather than consumer temptation knew true values. To work this unforgiving land, to live in so primitive a home, was to enjoy a satisfaction that a millionaire in the Madrid Ritz could not guess existed . . . His enthusiasm began to wane. It had to be admitted that modern living had softened every man until only the committed anchorite cheerfully rejected all comfort.

A dog came out of the house and stood, watching him, then began to bark. Munar came round the corner of the house. He gave an order and the dog retreated.

'Miguel?' Alvarez asked.

Munar, as always, neither confirmed nor denied that fact. A man could condemn himself as easily with words as actions.

'I'm Enrique, Dolores's cousin.'

He chewed his lower lip, scratched his neck, rubbed his stubbled chin, continued to stare vacantly at nothing.

'She suggested I drive over and have a chat with you.'

'Ain't you in the Cuerpo?'

'That's right. But I'm here as a relation, not because of my job.'

'Didn't ask you to come.'

'Dolores did because Luisa seems to be so worried.'

'Ain't no business of hers.'

Dolores might have warned him that Munar was this surly and unfriendly. 'I'm not here officially,' Alvarez continued patiently. 'It's a private visit to find out if there's anything I can do to help.'

'There ain't.'

The dog, tail down, approached them, then quickly retreated as Munar shouted at it. A lamb began to bleat and a sheep answered; the lamb rushed towards it, almost falling as it momentarily lost its footing.

Munar, feet splayed outwards because of the hours spent behind a mule-drawn plough, turned and, without a word, made for the house. Alvarez followed him indoors and up the stairs.

He slumped down in the nearer armchair and stared vacantly at the far wall. Alvarez sat on the second, equally uncomfortable armchair. This poorly furnished room evoked memories of his youth. His parents had never suffered outright poverty, but nor had they ever enjoyed the lightest touch of prosperity – which had meant anything not essential to the needs of just living – and their few pieces of furniture had remained in use until only fit for firewood . . .

Luisa came through the far doorway. A year younger than Munar, she looked older; her face was more lined, her skin more weathered, and, in contrast to his thick, wiry hair, her light brown hair was noticeably thin at the crown. Her body was hunched from years spent in the fields, irrigating, tilling, planting, harvesting. Her clothes were clean, but patched, shapeless, and sun-bleached almost colourless. She came to a stop in the middle of the room, began to fiddle with a button on her dress.

'I'm Enrique,' Alvarez said. 'Dolores suggested—'

'You tell her to mind her own business in future,' Munar said roughly. 'We don't need no help.'

'Yes, we do,' Luisa said.

'No, we bloody don't,' he shouted.

She faced him and it became obvious that there were times when she would stand up for herself however hard he tried to bully her. 'The sargento keeps saying he won't stop coming here until you're in jail.'

'Like all his kind, he's full of rollo.'

'Maybe, but he's still a sargento in the Guardia.'

'Tell me something I don't know . . . Don't matter what he is, he ain't got nothing on me.'

Alvarez said: 'He must think he has because he keeps returning to question you.'

'Ain't nothing better to do.'

'Someone's denounced my Miguel,' she said.

'Have you any idea who?'

'D'you think the bastard would still be walking on two legs if—' Miguel stopped as he belatedly realized this was not a question to put to a member of the Cuerpo even when not on duty.

'What's the denunciation claim?' Alvarez asked.

She waited for her husband to answer; finally, she said: 'There's been smuggling at Cala Balera.'

'And Miguel's been named as part of the gang?'

'I suppose.'

'What's being smuggled?'

'They ain't said, so how the bloody hell would she know?' Munar demanded violently.

'If the Guardia's so concerned, it's likely drugs.'

'You think I'd touch that shit?'

'If you've had nothing to do with what's been going on, I can't see it matters what you would or wouldn't handle.'

Munar clenched his fists.

The other's anger at the inference he might handle drugs had seemed genuine, Alvarez judged. 'What questions does the sargento ask?'

Because Munar did not answer, Luisa said: 'He wants to know where he was a fortnight ago on the Wednesday evening.'

'Presumably that's broadly when the goods were being landed. Has he ever mentioned a definite time?'

'Something like half eight.'

'Keep your tongue still,' Munar demanded roughly.

'Cala Balera is just over the mountains from here?' Alvarez waited.

'Maybe,' Munar finally answered, as if the exact where-abouts of the bay was doubtful.

'And there's no road, so it can only be reached on foot or by boat. How long would it take to walk from there to here?'

'Can't say.'

'Even a fit young man wouldn't do it in a hurry. So if you could prove you were here at half-past eight, you'd likely be all right despite the denunciation.'

'I told the sargento he was here all evening,' Luisa said. 'He was working the land; I held a sheep whilst he dagged it. But the sargento wouldn't believe me.'

'I'm afraid he was probably reckoning that a good wife will always do the best she can for her husband.'

'It's the truth.'

'I'm sure it is, but it'll need something more to persuade the sargento to stop worrying the two of you. Was there anyone else who might have seen Miguel here at around that time?'

'The foreigner.'

'The bastard sargento didn't believe that either,' Munar said with fresh anger.

'Tell me about him.'

'And waste me breath?'

'It comes free until one's dead.'

Munar spoke in jerky, often unfinished sentences. The foreigner had driven up in a car . . . What did it matter what kind of bloody car? . . . Small, green, looked new . . . Make? Could've been anything . . . The man had climbed out of the car and walked across to where he'd been working . . . Describe him? Next he'd be asked if the man had twelve toes. Not nearly as old as Alvarez . . . 'You look more than that' . . . 'All I'm saying is, you look older than you tell' . . . Black hair, round face, pointed chin, too slightly built to be any good in the field, and a slight limp . . . Height? Maybe one metre eighty . . . Dressed like any tourist – open-neck shirt, trousers, sandals . . . He'd walked across and tried to speak in Castilian and sounded like he'd got a twisted tongue. He'd returned to the car and brought out a small book that had questions in Castilian and English. He wanted to find someone . . . As he'd told the sargento enough times for even that lump of cow dung to understand, he couldn't remember the name; it was a foreign one, English like as not, but that's all he could say. The sargento had called him a poor liar. The other's mother had to be pitied for bearing such a disbelieving bastard of a son.

The sargento might not have believed an Englishman had visited the farm on the Wednesday evening, but Alvarez judged that that was probably the truth. When Munar lied, his lie would be of a 'concrete' nature; what he had just described had an insubstantial air.

Luisa said: 'If the Englishman told the sargento he's spoken to Miguel, would that stop all our trouble?'

'If the times coincided,' Alvarez answered evasively, 'it would prove Miguel could not have been in Cala Balera when the cargo was being unloaded.'

24

'Then you must find him.'

'Unless Miguel can remember his name, that will be very difficult, perhaps impossible.'

She turned to face her husband. 'Remember!'

'How can I, woman?' he shouted. 'He spoke so bad the name could've been anything.'

'Then you'll have to—'

'Do nothing,' he said angrily.

She hesitated, looking at her husband with an expression suggesting doubt, then turned to Alvarez. 'We'll pay you to find the Englishman.'

'With what, when we ain't no money?' Munar demanded.

'There's no question of paying me,' Alvarez said. 'Are there many foreigners living in the valley?'

'Only one,' she answered. 'A German bought the estate at the head and now stops anyone walking through his land on the old mule track to the next valley.'

'Since I don't walk over no mountains,' Munar said loudly, 'that don't worry me.'

She appealed to Alvarez. 'You'll find the Englishman so as the sargento can't take Miguel to prison?'

'I'll do everything possible,' he answered. The assurance would keep her happy; if she were happy, Dolores would have no cause for complaint – or reason for sandwich suppers. 'I'd better be on my way now.'

'You'll not go before you've wet your tongue,' she said firmly. She hurried out of the room.

He could be certain he would be offered home-made wine, so dark it would resemble earth in colour as well as taste. An oenophile would name it worse than the lees from an Andaluce bodega, but he would enjoy it; as did this room, it would remind him of his youth.

When she returned, she carried a tin tray on which were three glasses, a jug of water, several cubes of ice in a plastic bowl, and a bottle that clearly did not contain home-made wine. She put the tray down on the table.

'What have you got there?' Munar shouted with angry consternation.

'Whisky.'

He swore violently. Then, noticing Alvarez's interest, tried to calm himself. 'Maybe he don't like whisky.'

She asked Alvarez: 'D'you want some?'

'It's one of my favourite drinks,' he assured her.

'What d'you want with it?'

'Just ice.'

She poured out a large drink, added ice, passed him the glass. He drank. The taste – silky smooth, with a hint of some hidden quality that intrigued the palate – was like none he had enjoyed before. 'This is something special!'

As she handed her husband a glass, she said: 'It's twenty-year-old malt.'

'No, it ain't,' Munar hurriedly corrected her. 'It's ordinary cheap whisky.'

Neither cheap nor ordinary, Alvarez decided as he enjoyed another mouthful. It was astonishing to be offered such quality in surroundings so spartan.

The same thought was obviously in Munar's mind. He cleared his throat. 'Jorge gave it to me.'

'Jorge?'

'Our youngest,' she explained. She settled on the settee.

'Always gives me something real good on me Saint's Day,' Munar said.

Within a remarkably short time, Alvarez noted, the whisky had changed from being cheap and ordinary to real good.

'Never forgets, Jorge doesn't. Isn't that right?'

She nodded.

'A bottle every Saint's Day and at Christmas. He's a real

good lad. It's not every son gives his father such presents. Never forgets. Every Saint's Day.'

The partridge, Alvarez thought, which scuttled away, trailing its wings as if wounded, was trying to draw attention away from its brood; Munar preferred to try to save himself. 'Dolores says you've two sons.'

She answered. Two strong, handsome sons: Jorge in Madrid, Mario in Salamanca. They lived in large houses and drove big cars; were married to beautiful women; Jorge had two sons, Mario a daughter. Lovely children. Only she didn't see them as often as she'd like. Julia and Carolina didn't enjoy coming to the island. And even when they did, they stayed at the Hotel Parelona and only occasionally brought the grandchildren to the finca.

It was what she hadn't said that painted the relationships for Alvarez. He could be certain the two wives did not wish to be reminded of their husbands' background. Prosperity bred snobbism.

'Would you like another drink?' she asked.

He was surprised to find his glass was empty.

As he drove down the dirt track to the road, he was thankful smuggling was not his concern. Let the sargento wonder whether a son so weak he allowed his wife to dictate his relationship with his parents would bother to remember his father's Saint's Day; and remembering, would send a bottle of whisky that would cost goodness knows how many bottles of Soberano. Let him hear Munar's repeated affirmations of his son's generosity and wonder why a man normally so taciturn should suddenly become so voluble.

He reached the road and turned right, making for the head of the valley. That bottle of malt whisky, and many more, had been landed at Cala Balera on the Wednesday evening. Since Munar probably had been on his farm at the time, it could be assumed he was the guardian – somewhere on his land was a very well-hidden cave in which the contraband could be stored until it could be safely distributed.

Since he was an officer of the law, a pedant would hold he should pass on what he had learned to the Guardia. But he was an islander and therefore accepted that smuggling innocent items, such as malt whisky, was certainly no crime, more a way of life . . .

As he neared the head of the valley, the mountains on either side began to close and inexplicably one side was bare rock, on the other pine trees grew in some profusion. He approached a gateway, with large, elaborate wrought-iron gates, mechanically controlled, from either side of which stretched a high stone wall, the light shades of stone wherever this had been shaped showing the walls had been newly built. On the right-hand side of the gate was a notice in German, English, French, and Castilian, informing would-be pedestrians that there was no public right of way. One more part of the island denied to those to whom it truly belonged. By the side of the notice was a speaker-box with a call button. He climbed out of the car, pressed the button. A man's voice, sounding very tinny, asked him what he wanted. 'Cuerpo General de Policia,' he answered. The gates swung open, to the accompaniment of considerable mechanical noise.

He drove along a well-maintained, metalled road bordered by trim, newly mown grass that was green, indicating constant watering. Water that towns like Llueso lacked. The road made a sharp turn and he came in sight of a manorial house, four floors high with an inner courtyard. There were not many such mansions – there had never been a large, wealthy aristocracy who had either lived on, or frequently visited, the island – and because of the cost of repairs, these were often in poor condition; this one could hardly have been in better. As he left the car and looked up at the steep roofs, many windows, and grandiloquent portico, he wondered how many millions of pesetas had been spent on restoration? And to afford to spend that much, a man had to have many, many more millions. He did not normally suffer jealousy, but to own such a piece of history and all the land that accompanied it . . .

He climbed the six marble steps, rang the bell to the side of the heavy wooden door that was striated and greyed by age. Almost immediately, the door was opened by a man in his mid-twenties. 'What's the problem?' he asked aggressively.

There had been a time when a policeman met only respect; democracy did have a downside. 'Is the owner here?'

'He's in Frankfurt; been there since last month.'

'So who would have been in this house on Wednesday, the seventh?'

'Why d'you want to know?'

'To find out if anyone called during the evening.'

The other, discovering he was not directly involved, relaxed. 'When Señor Heine's away, there's always someone has to be around on account of insurance – there's a lot of valuable stuff.'

'Then were you here that Wednesday evening?'

'I suppose. Most Wednesdays, Inés goes and sees her mother and I'm on my own.'

'Did an Englishman come here during the evening, asking if someone he named lived here?'

'That's right.'

'Tell me about it.'

'I was watching the telly when the gate buzzer sounded. I spoke to him over the line. He tried Spanish but I couldn't understand a word, so I asked if he spoke English. He wanted to know if someone he mentioned lived here.'

'What name did he give?'

'Can't remember.'

'It would help a great deal if you could try to.'

After a while, he said: 'I guess it was something like Perez.'

'How like would you reckon?'

'Maybe it was Perez,' was his indirect answer. 'Only that don't sound English, does it?'

'Not really.'

'Can't do better than that . . . Anyway, I told him this was Señor Heine's place. Then he cleared off.'

'So you never saw him?'

'No.'

Alvarez thanked the other, returned to his car, and drove off. He had learned that a foreigner, probably an Englishman, had been in the valley that Wednesday evening, but there was no certainty, only the very strong probability, that he was the same man whom Munar claimed had spoken to him. The person being sought did not live in Exchau Valley, his name was something like Perez. He might be staying anywhere on the island or might already have left and returned home. Clearly, there was nothing more which could be done to help Munar establish his 'innocence'.

Four

Alvarez returned home knowing he had done all that a mortal man could do. Dolores, reasonable when not in one of her female moods, would accept this and would not blame him for failing to achieve the impossible.

He parked, walked along the pavement to their house and unlocked the front door – something that would have been unnecessary thirty years before. The front room was, as ever, spotlessly clean and tidy; in the dining/sitting-room, Jaime was watching television, seated within reasonable reach of a bottle of Soberano.

As Alvarez began to pour himself a drink, Dolores stepped through the bead curtain. 'You're back.'

He agreed he was back; he did not give himself as large a drink as he would have done had she remained in the kitchen.

'Have you spoken to Luisa and Miguel?'

'I'm just back from seeing them.'

'So everything has been sorted out and Luisa has no need to worry any more.'

He spoke carefully. 'I'm afraid it's not quite that simple.'

Her expression sharpened; she folded her arms across her chest. 'What does that mean?'

He dropped three ice cubes into the brandy. 'There are problems.'

'Such as what?'

'It's very possible Miguel knows a lot more about the smuggling than he should.'

'Why do you say that?'

'It's the way he spoke. And because when Luisa asked me if I'd like a drink—'

'An unnecessary question.'

'—she came back into the room with a bottle of twenty-year-old malt whisky.'

'You've been boozing that?' Jaime said enviously. 'If you ask me—'

'No one has asked you anything,' Dolores snapped. She turned back to Alvarez. 'You accepted their kind hospitality, yet call them liars?'

'Miguel was obviously furious she'd produced the bottle and scared I'd start thinking; which I did.'

'Nonsense!'

'If you weren't there—'

'Perhaps I was not, but I have a far more balanced judgment than you. No doubt, you choose to believe this stupidity to provide an excuse for doing nothing more.'

'Well, I don't. For your information, they told me an Englishman had called at their place, looking for someone, at a time which would have made it impossible for Miguel to have been engaged in the actual smuggling operation. But although the Englishman had introduced himself, Miguel couldn't begin to remember the name; any more than he could tell me anything else about the man. To identify one foreigner amongst all the tens of thousands on the island when no one knows his name is virtually an impossibility. Nevertheless, certain what all this meant to you, I promised myself I'd continue. I drove up to the head of the valley where a German has bought the manorial estate to find out if the Englishman had been there, because that would provide confirmation of Miguel's story. One of the servants was in the house and he told me that an Englishman had called, but he hadn't seen him and had only spoken to him through the speaker at the gates. He thought the name was something like Perez, but was far from certain. That's all he could tell me. So despite all my hard work, I learned nothing.' He finished his drink. 'And without any definite, established facts to go on, it really is impossible to identify him.'

'You know his name sounds like Perez.'

'How like? How many tourists on the island have names which sound sufficiently similar . . . ?'

'Find out.'

'To do that, I'd have to study every registration card of every person staying at a hotel, identify every tourist who is not staying in a hotel and so has not made out a card . . .'

'Which you won't start doing all the time you're sitting there, drinking.'

'Can't you understand—?'

'I understand that you are unwilling to do anything more to help Luisa.'

'Be reasonable . . . I've done everything possible.'

'That is unfortunate.'

The threat was unmistakable. 'Officially, I can't ask for any action because Salas would have to agree to it; and to carry out a search of that magnitude on my own would be like trying to push a pea up Puig Major with my nose.'

'As you wish.' She turned and swept through the bead curtain into the kitchen.

Jaime poured himself another drink. 'You've really messed things up. Couldn't try to help Cousin Luisa, could you?'

'Haven't you been listening?'

'To what? You trying to make out you've not been sitting on your arse?'

'If you'd done half as much as I have, you'd now be

totally exhausted and in intensive care.' Had he really been such a fool as earlier to think things would be all right? Look for gratitude only from those who are in your debt. Now, thanks to female lack of logic, Dolores was once again threatening them with a life of sackcloth, ashes, and sandwiches. Clearly, if a catastrophe was to be avoided, he was going to have to sacrifice himself further. He finished his drink, went through to the kitchen.

Dolores was pounding something in a mortar with such vigour she was sweating freely. Her hair was in some disarray, there was a smudge of flour on one cheek, her apron was patched and faded, but when she straightened up, she regarded him with so fierce and scornful a pride, she might have been in silks and he in rags.

'I've been thinking,' he said humbly.

She resumed work. The pungent scent of crushed garlic was strong.

'The Englishman was looking for someone whose name was something like Perez.'

'So you said.'

'Since only Miguel and the German are in Exchau Valley, he can't live there.'

'You have already drunk so much that you find the obvious interesting?'

'It's no good to start looking for someone unless you can be reasonably certain where he's likely to be living. There's only one road to Exchau Valley and that also gives access to Almerich Valley. So I reckon it's possible he mistook the valley he wanted and, having found that out, continued on to Almerich. If I'm right, there will be someone in that valley whose name can be mistaken for Perez and he'll be able to identify the Englishman who'll confirm he spoke to Miguel at a time which makes it impossible Miguel was in Cala Balera, working contraband. If that fails, there's another possibility. Assume he's a tourist, then the car he was driving was almost certainly hired. I can contact all the car hire firms and get them to search for a recent customer of that name or something which sounds similar.'

She lifted up the pestle and used a knife to scrape the crushed garlic off it. 'My grandmother used to say that a man's mind was like a sponge; it had to be squeezed to find out what was in it.'

He had never met her grandmother; there was reason to be grateful that this was so.

Almerich Valley ran roughly parallel to Exchau Valley, but was much larger. Its soil contained fewer stones and rocks, but was only slightly more fertile and in the past several families who had lived along its length had known only hard work and small returns. Then the foreigners had 'discovered' it. They had not seen sour, unproductive land, but somewhere quiet and peaceful within relatively easy reach of the coast, yet beyond the baleful influence of tourists. Not understanding that a Mallorquin never committed himself to the sale of anything without prolonged and tortured thought – was he asking every last peseta the miserly bastard would pay; was the miserly bastard putting one over him? – the foreigners who tried to buy property had regarded continuing equivocation as a sign that they were not offering enough and had increased the amount. As each Mallorquin family had left, having been paid many times what they had optimistically thought possible, they had given thanks to the Good Lord who had ensured there were many foreign fools in the world.

Some of the old stone houses had been demolished and replaced with large, luxurious villas, some had been so altered and enlarged that their character was lost; it was difficult to decide which type of building was the more anomalous in a valley whose nature, formed by the soil and surrounding mountains, was one of harsh austerity.

The first home was a U-shaped bungalow. Alvarez stepped out of his car on to the circular drive and as he walked towards the three marble steps which gave access to the porch, wondered whether Dolores could be persuaded to appreciate the extent of his sacrifice? Saturday morning was a time for looking forward to Saturday afternoon and Sunday, not for working hard . . . He rang the front door bell and the door was opened by a middle-aged woman who wore an apron. He introduced himself. 'You may be able to help me. Do you know anyone who lives in this valley whose name sounds like Perez?'

'No,' she answered curtly.

'Who lives in this house?'

'Señor and Señora Lodge.'

'Are they here now?'

'The señora is.'

'I'd like a word with her.'

'Then you're the only one.'

He followed her through a luxuriously furnished sitting-room and out on to the patio. Beyond the southern side of the large, oval-shaped swimming pool was a complex of changing rooms, open area, and barbecue. A woman lay on the chaise-longue within the shade of the open area. As he drew closer, her age increased; he decided that she would have been very well advised to wear a bathing costume that covered considerably more of her tired flesh.

'Is Inspector Alvarez,' said the maid in heavily accented English.

'Who?'

He answered. 'I am a member of the Cuerpo General de Policia, señora.'

'What does that mean?' She spoke in the high-pitched,

strangulated-vowelled voice of a woman who wished to be thought a lady. Reflective sunglasses hid her eyes, but the set of her thin lips suggested more of her character than she would have wished.

'I am a detective.'

She picked up a glass from the low table by her side and drank.

No Mallorquin would have had the ill manners to drink in front of him without asking what he would like. 'I am hoping you will be able to help me, señora.'

'Most unlikely.'

'I am trying to trace someone, probably English, whose name is perhaps Perez.'

'Either it is or it isn't.' She put the glass down on the table.

'I cannot be certain.'

'I suggest you remedy that uncertainty before you trouble anyone else.'

'The name was spoken by an Englishman to a Mallorquin and it can be difficult to understand precisely in another language. It is possible the person lives in this valley.'

'Then suppose you leave and find out if he does?'

It would have been a pleasure to try to match her rudeness, but some pleasures came too expensively. About to reply politely, his attention was caught by the sound of a door being shut. He looked towards the house. A man, dressed in smart casual clothes, crossed the patio and walked around the pool. 'Morning,' he said, with bluff good humour, as he came to a stop. 'Lovely day.'

'It is indeed, señor.'

'Thank God you speak English! So many people here don't – can't understand why not. Rosa says you're a policeman. I plead guilty.' He chuckled.

'Control yourself devant les domestiques,' she snapped.

'Rosa's in the kitchen – getting the meal ready, I suppose.'

'Il pense qu'il parle la langue Anglaise.'

'Then maybe he's learned to enjoy a bit of humour.'

'Hardly relevant.'

'But when I said—'

'Quite.'

'Oh, very well. By the by, the French windows were open, letting all the cold air out.'

She turned to Alvarez. 'When one is trying hard to keep a house cool with very expensive air-conditioning – electricity doesn't cost nearly as much in England – it hardly helps to leave an outside door open.'

'I think, señora, the maid returned inside after I first spoke to you . . .'

'Being a local, she's stupid, but she has learned to shut doors.'

'But—'

'In my country, it's bad manners to argue.'

'The room will soon cool down again,' Lodge said, in conciliatory tones. 'D'you know if Rosa has put more tonic in the frig out here?'

'I told her to, which probably means she hasn't.'

'I'll look.'

'You can get me another drink.'

He went forward and picked up the glass from the table. 'What's your poison?'

'Must you always be facetious? I want a small whisky and plenty of ginger ale.'

He walked through the open area to the small sideboard and large refrigerator at the back.

'Marie rang while you were out,' she said. 'We're asked to dinner on Monday. I couldn't make up my mind whether to suggest that whoever else they invited, not the Duggans.'

'And did you?'

'In the end, no. But I'm sure I should have done. You can't really blame Marie with her come-from, but she has no social nous and seems ready to ask everyone.'

Lodge came forward and handed his wife a glass, passed Alvarez and sat on one of the canvas and aluminium chairs. 'Bottoms up.' He raised his glass.

'Can you never remember how much I detest that vulgarity?'

'Afraid I'll use it when Ian's around and he'll become over-excited?'

'Enough!'

They drank. She looked at Alvarez. 'Is there some reason for your continuing to stand there?'

She had not had the courtesy to ask him to sit. 'Señora, I should like to ask the señor if he knows someone who lives in the valley whose name sounds like Perez.'

'I have already answered that there is no one.'

'Hang on, old girl,' Lodge said. 'If you stop and think about it, Perez does sound something like Perry.'

'Not if the names are pronounced correctly.'

'Would a native ever do that?'

Native as with hide shield and hand-forged spear? Alvarez said: 'There is someone who lives in this valley whose name is Perry?'

'Rented a place a little time back, so we've got to know them,' Lodge answered.

'We have met them,' she corrected.

'Met them, then. Truth to tell, I don't think they're as bad as you find them.'

'A gentleman does not behave as he did at Roper's cocktail party.'

'Gabriella was leading him on.'

'Being a man, you naturally try to excuse him like that.'

39

'Dammit, haven't you heard her saying often enough that sailing is a complete bore because it takes ten times as long to get half as far? Yet she was telling Basil how much she'd like a trip in his yacht.' Lodge chuckled. 'If he does take her out, he won't want Iris keeping an eye on the sheets.'

'Must you be crude?'

'You don't think that's rather witty? Twisted sheets are one thing on deck, something very different in the cabin . . .'

'There is no need to explain.'

Alvarez said: 'Señor, can you tell me where Señor Perry lives?'

'He's renting Colin's place, which must make Colin very happy since the money's enough to keep him in brandy for years.'

'That is a canard,' she snapped. 'Colin comes from a very good family.'

'Then he's almost guaranteed to drink like a fish.'

A refined lady did not swear in company, otherwise she undoubtedly would have done so.

'Where is the house?' Alvarez asked.

'Last place up the valley,' Lodge answered.

'Then I will drive there. Thank you, señor, thank you, señora, for your help.'

Lodge nodded, she ignored his words.

His car, having been in the full sun, was hot enough to serve as an antechamber to hell. The Lodges' car, or cars, would have air-conditioning. Money might not make for happiness, but it certainly guaranteed comfort. He started the engine, but did not immediately drive off. He was faced with a problem. Because he had left Llueso later than intended, and questioning the Lodges had taken longer than expected, the hour was late. Yet logically, the sensible thing now was to drive up the valley to the rented house and find out if the occupants were the people the unknown Englishman had been seeking. However, do that and he might well arrive home too late to enjoy a couple of iced brandies before the meal, a failure that would exacerbate the suffering the Lodges had inflicted on him. There were times when logic failed to signpost the logical course to take. When he drove through the gateway, he turned right.

Five

A s Alvarez drove towards Almerich Valley for the second time that day, he had reason to be bitter. Had he not succumbed to the sybaritic siren which plagued every man, he would have completed his work that morning and would now be resting. Had Dolores . . . He'd carefully explained to her why he'd not yet found out if the Englishman had called at the Perry's house that Wednesday evening, he'd assured her that a delay until Monday was far from critical since clearly the Guardia did not have enough evidence to arrest Miguel, he'd sworn that if there were the slightest risk, he would rush . . . Women enjoyed leading emotional lives. She had expressed her vicarious distress and who could tell how much more that would torment her if he did not return to the valley after the briefest of siestas . . .

He passed a field in which a small flock of red sheep – an island breed in danger of extinction – were lethargically searching for something to eat when experience should have taught them there was nothing. Summer was a hard time for animals. He could still remember his father's despair when he had had to slaughter the few sheep and lambs he possessed because there was no feed on the ground and he had no money to buy any, and although they might have survived until the rains returned, he would not let them experience the suffering that that must entail. His father had had too much empathy for the welfare of both animals and humans. In those hard days, that had been a weakness, not a strength.

He passed between the two bluffs that marked the mouth of the valley and for the second time that day marvelled at the majesty of the mountains whose crests pierced the blue sky; looking up through the windscreen, he saw a black vulture, riding the thermals with outstretched wings. He wondered if the Lodges ever appreciated the grandeur of their surroundings? Perhaps he might, but for her, nature would be insufficiently well-bred to be considered.

He reached the head of the valley and the last house. This had obviously been reformed and enlarged but, exceptionally, this had been done with sufficient sympathy for the past and it was still possible to discern that it had once been a typical Mallorquin farmhouse. He approved of the surrounding garden since the geraniums in earthenware pots needed little attention, the bushes, even less, the century cacti, none at all.

He crossed to the house. Heavy, crude wooden doors were swung open and beyond were modern wooden and glass doors. Since foreigners lived here, he did not enter and call out, but knocked and waited.

Through the glass, he saw a woman, for whom middle age was fact, not threat, cross the tiled floor. Black, curly hair framed a round, regular face that was pleasantly, but far from strikingly, featured. She wasn't plump, nor was she scrawny; her clothes bore the stamp of good taste.

She opened the door. 'Good afternoon,' she said in heavily accented Spanish.

'Good afternoon, señora,' he replied in English. Lines in her face suggested a stronger character that he had first judged; her generous lips possessed that curve which male legend held was a sure sign of a passionate nature . . .

He hurriedly checked his thoughts. 'My name is Inspector Alvarez, Cuerpo General de Policia.'

She stared at him for several seconds, then said, her voice strained: 'You . . . you're a policeman?'

'Yes, señora.' He smiled. 'But please don't think there has been any trouble.' It amused him that the English so respected the law, their consciences never slept – let them park on a blue line and not buy a ticket and a sense of guilt pursued them. No Mallorquin normally bought a parking ticket and if this omission was discovered by authority, he suffered only a sense of outrage at his ill fortune. 'I merely wish to ask if an Englishman called here just over a couple of weeks ago?'

'Oh!' She hesitated, then said: 'I'm sorry, leaving you standing there, but I was trying to remember what I could possibly have done wrong. Please come in.'

How onerous the English must find an honest life! He stepped inside.

'We're just about to have a drink, so will you join us?'

'With pleasure, señora.' The difference between the nature of his reception now and in the morning could hardly have been greater, but then Señora Lodge had iced bile – blue – running through her veins . . .

'If you'll come through.'

He entered a large, oblong room with high, beamed ceiling, which had almost certainly been a barn. The over-head light – eight bulbs set on a circle of wrought-iron – was switched on because otherwise the room would have been dim, despite the brilliant sunshine outside, as there was only one small window; old rock walls were very thick and often their cores were merely loose stones so that to breach them was always difficult and if too large a hole was made, there was the danger the wall would collapse.

44

'If you'd say what you'd like to drink, I'll ask my husband to pour it.'

'May I have a coñac, please, with just ice.'

'I won't be a moment.' She went through the far doorway.

The room was simply furnished – a couple of low, glass-topped tables, a bookcase, a locally made sideboard on which stood a couple of highly polished copper coffee pots, a brightly-coloured, circular carpet, three armchairs and a settee in matching loose covers, television and video, and, on the walls, three paintings of local scenes – olive trees, caseta, mountains, cove, sea – and one of a yacht with crimson hull under spinnaker and mainsail.

He sat on one of the armchairs. From beyond the doorway came the murmur of voices. Languages possessed different rhythms which could sometimes identify them even when the words could not be distinguished. English was the murmur of the sea, Dutch, the constant clearing of the throat, Italian, raw emotion . . .

The far door opened and the woman returned, followed by her husband who carried a tray. Alvarez, remembering that odd English custom, stood.

'Hullo, there.' Perry put the tray down on the nearer occasional table, came forward and smiled as he shook hands. 'Glad you could join us in a sundowner – one of life's more civilized habits.' He picked up a glass from the tray, handed it across. 'If you'd like more brandy or ice, just shout.'

'Thank you, señor.' The grey hair and moustache marked Perry as older than Alvarez would otherwise have judged. Well built, handsome in a rugged fashion, with a ready smile, he projected an immediate friendliness; and on further judgment, the suggestion of a degree of libidinousness. Perhaps Señora Lodge had not been so wrong as her husband had maintained . . .

'Please sit. And good health to all.'

He sat. He drank. The coñac could be Carlos I or perhaps Torres Hors d'Age. Whichever, if one had to work on a Saturday afternoon because of an irrational female there were compensations to be enjoyed.

Perry said: 'I gather you want to know if someone called here the other day?'

'A couple of weeks ago, on Wednesday night or more likely on the Thursday or Friday.'

'Are we allowed to know why the interest?'

'A man who is suspected of having been engaged in a criminal activity claims that at a specific time he was at home. When asked to corroborate that, he remembered that a foreigner, almost certainly an Englishman, called at his home and asked if he knew where another Englishman lived. The suspect cannot remember the name that was mentioned. I have spoken to someone else who was also approached by an Englishman that evening and he recalls the name Perez. There was reason to think the person sought might be living in this valley and this morning I asked Señora Lodge if she could help me—'

'On bended knees, I trust?'

For the sake of good public relations, Alvarez merely smiled. 'She couldn't. But Señor Lodge returned and he suggested "Perez" might be mistaken for "Perry", which is why I am here now. If indeed an Englishman did call, I should like to identify him to learn if he can corroborate the evidence of the suspect.'

'Naturally, we'd help if we could, but I'm afraid that we'd sailed over to Menorca and so weren't here.'

'Has anyone been in touch with you since then?'

'Someone we don't know or didn't expect – no.'

'Then it's obviously a coincidence that the name of the person the Englishman was seeking sounded like yours.'

'Basil, aren't you forgetting . . .' she began.

'What am I forgetting?'

'That Matilde said an Englishman had called here on the Thursday.'

'Darling, the inspector is referring to what happened relatively recently. Matilde told us about the Englishman weeks ago.'

'It wasn't all that long.'

'The experts say time is relative; with you, it's relatively relative! Remember when you swore we'd had dinner with the Lowerys only a week before and it turned out to be a month?'

'There were special reasons for my mixing things up.'

'Aren't there always?'

'No, there aren't. And this time—'

'Let's leave the argument for later when we don't have a guest to bore.'

'But . . .' she began, then became silent.

Alvarez said: 'Señor, do I understand that an Englishman whom you didn't know or weren't expecting did call here?'

'Many weeks ago – with great respect to my beloved wife – we returned for lunch to be told by Matilde – our daily – that while we'd been out, a man had turned up and seemed to want to talk to us. I say "seemed" because her English has to be heard to be believed and the odds are that neither of them understood a single word the other was saying. He never returned and so probably he was on holiday, slightly bored, and, having met us somewhere in England, suffered the presumption we'd like to meet him again.'

'Was he English?'

'According to Matilde, he spoke English to her. We have French friends, but they naturally insist they can't speak a

word of English . . . Your glass is empty. Let me refill it.'
He stood.

Alvarez held out his glass and Perry took it before turning
to his wife. 'Do you know if there's more gin? I finished the
bottle just now.'

'I bought three more yesterday.'

'Where did you put them?'

'Where you keep the gin, of course.'

'I couldn't see them.'

'Try looking.'

He chuckled. 'When a wife can't find something, it's been
moved; when a husband can't, he hasn't looked. My sweet,
I assure you that wherever you did put the bottles, it wasn't
on the normal shelf. Come and show me where they are.'

'But—'

'I promise not to jeer when you find you've put them
somewhere odd.'

They left.

Alvarez heard their talking, his voice a murmur, hers
initially louder and then as subdued as his – the words
were indecipherable. The talking ceased and moments later,
she returned, sat. 'They weren't where I meant them to be
because there was a phone call and I just put them down
quickly, but half a proper look would have shown him where
they are.'

Her face was slightly flushed. Because of annoyance? She
used her forefinger to stroke the right-hand side of her mouth
for a couple of seconds. Could there really be any truth in
the belief that lips shaped like hers . . .

'Do you like sailing?' she asked.

'I have only been out once in a yacht and then there was
too much wind. I was very sick.'

'An unfortunate initiation! . . . We do a lot of sailing.
That's our yacht, the *Argo* – no oracular beam, but still

somewhat special.' She pointed to the painting on the far wall.

'It looks very nice,' he said, mustering as much sincerity as possible.

'She's a Peller and Petterson forty-five footer . . . I'd never sailed before I met Basil and, to tell the truth, for a while I was quite scared, especially when the sea was rough. But he's being doing it since he was no age and is so skilful that very soon I learned to enjoy it every bit as much as he does. We had our honeymoon on her. That's why our marriage had a stormy beginning!'

He smiled his appreciation of her joke.

Perry returned, passed a glass to his wife and to Alvarez, sat.

'I've been telling the inspector how much we enjoy sailing,' she said.

'Very true. And, in fact, that's what brought us here in the first place and why we've decided to stay a while – the facilities are first class.'

'You sound as if you do not intend to remain here?' Alvarez said.

'We rented this place on a short lease as we could then make up our minds whether to settle or sail on. Maybe we'll put down our roots, maybe we won't. As for so many yachtsmen, for me – but perhaps not so much for Iris – the perfect berth is always just beyond the horizon. Are you a wanderer?'

'No, señor. I prefer to be settled.'

'I'm not surprised, living on this peach of an island.'

How typical! Alvarez thought. Perry could afford to enjoy any lifestyle, but obviously wasn't able to decide which one he wanted; here he was, knowing exactly what he wanted – many hectares of fertile land with wells that never dried up – yet lacking the money to turn dreams into reality.

'I presume you live nearby?' Perry said.

'In Llueso.'

'Where we often stop off on our way to or from the port. It's a very attractive town.'

But for how much longer? Alvarez mentally sighed. However much one sought to preserve the past, and even the present, the future belonged to the peseta (and one day soon, that illegitimate monstrosity, the euro). He finished his drink, stood. 'Thank you for your help.'

'Glad to be able to give it and just sorry it was of no use,' Perry replied.

Iris remained in the sitting-room, Perry accompanied him to the front door. 'Don't hesitate to come back if you think there's anything more we can do for you.'

He settled behind the wheel of his Ibiza, drove out on to the road and headed south. When he'd announced himself, Iris had seemingly been dismayed, even shocked. Merely evidence of a typical English conscience? When she had mentioned how Matilde had told them about an Englishman who had called, her husband had been quick to suggest this had happened long before she judged. When he had said he could not find the gin, he had insisted she show him where it was – when in the kitchen, the rhythm of their voices could have suggested disagreement. Had he persuaded her into the kitchen on a trumped-up reason in order to say something that could not be said in the sitting-room? Something concerning the Englishman who had called? Had her estimate of time been more accurate than his? . . . He cut short the questions. Only a philosopher troubled his brain with problems of no practical consequence.

Dolores would have to accept that Miguel's last hope was

that no more adverse evidence would come to light (and he should move the whisky beyond his wife's impetuous reach). If only he knew how to make Dolores accept anything.

Six

Nothing could change the fact that Monday was Monday and midday Saturday was five and a half days away. Alvarez looked down at the fax which had been put on his desk before his arrival and he wondered what was so important? If news was good, it matured, if bad, it was best ignored . . .

Judging it was merienda time, he looked at his watch and was dismayed to note there was still half an hour to go. Suppose, his thoughts ran, he left now and returned half an hour sooner than he would normally have done, where could be the harm? He made his way downstairs. The duty cabo said: 'Ever quicker off the mark, uncle!'

'The early bird eats well.'

'Eat much more and even outsize won't fit you.'

The country had gone to the dogs when the modern generation could be so incorrectly insolent. The street was thronged with tourists. The village no longer belonged to the Mallorquins. It had been overrun by foreigners who drank themselves stupid and women who dressed like putas.

He reached the old square, newly reformed. (Question. What is the one project at which the EU is invariably successful? Answer. Spending on irrational and unwanted projects.) He edged his way through the crowd to the Club Llueso.

'You're early,' the barman said.

'I've had a very stressful morning.'

'Who hasn't?'

'That lot out there.'

As he indicated the window, two young women in brief, very tight shorts walked past.

'There's some stress that's welcome,' the barman observed.

'At your age, it only leads to frustration.'

'Speak for yourself.'

'I'll have a coffee and a coñac and if your hand starts shaking when you're pouring, let it.' Alvarez crossed to one of the tables by a window and sat. It truly had been a stressful morning. 'The superior chief,' his secretary had said over the telephone, her plum-laden voice thick with assumed authority, 'requires to see your crime diary for the past six months and you will submit it by Friday.'

'I'll do my best . . .'

'By Friday.' The line went dead.

He'd replaced the receiver, wondering whether every inspector was being asked to submit his crime diary on some bureaucratic whim or had Superior Chief Salas targeted only him? He wondered exactly how a crime diary should be composed and executed?

The barman crossed and put coffee and a brandy on the table. Alvarez drank some of the brandy, some coffee, then tipped the remaining brandy into the cup. Crime diary! When did a busy inspector have time for that nonsense? . . . As the weeks, then the months, had passed and there had been no demand for sight of the diary, he had assumed that sanity had prevailed and the idea could be forgotten. He should have had the common sense to understand that governments and bureaucrats had little time for sanity . . . . 'I'll have another brandy.'

'One day you'll surprise me,' the bartender replied.

Even if it were possible to provide a chronologically

correct account of the last six months, the work involved would be horrendous. Yet Salas was a Madrileño and incapable of understanding such a fact; any fact, come to that. So was his only solution to fall ill? If he were away from work for long enough, the odds must be that the order finally would be forgotten. He knew a doctor who owed him a favour. A broken leg so that he couldn't move? But that wouldn't stop his sitting at a desk and writing. A broken right arm? Salas would demand he wrote with his left; if both arms, with his teeth. It had to be something stronger. Bubonic plague or Lassa fever?

The second brandy arrived and helped him decide he was being unnecessarily pessimistic. The unreliability of the postal service could be used to advantage since it was almost impossible to prove that something had not been posted (so long as it was not registered), and one of the men who worked in the Llueso post office owed him a favour.

He smoked a cigarette, finished the brandy, checked the time and was pleasantly surprised to find there were still ten minutes to go before he need return to the office. It was only after he'd left the Club Llueso that he remembered he'd arrived there half an hour early.

The telephone in his office was ringing. He sat and wished it into silence and after only one more ring it did become silent. He settled back in the chair. It was so hot that people were comparing this year with the infamous one fifty-three years before when cattle had died in the fields and wells which had hitherto always flowed dried up. To overwork in such heat was dangerous. His eyelids closed and he was enjoying the gentle slide into sleep when the phone rang again. He struggled into an upright position, reached out, and lifted the receiver.

'Where the devil have you been all morning?' Salas demanded.

'Señor, I was making inquiries . . .'

'Are you incapable of obeying orders?'

He was supposed to leave word of where he was going. 'I thought I'd only be away for a short time . . .'

'I wish I could decide once and for all whether your problem is incompetence or—'

'Of course, had I known—'

'—or deliberate disobedience.'

Someone had seen him enter the Club Llueso and stay there for longer than usual and had denounced him. If ever he identified who that had been . . . 'Señor, I had to enter the Club Llueso because there was reason to believe a possible witness was inside.'

'And you can somehow imagine that that excuses your actions?'

'But was I to stand outside the Club until either he left or it became clear my information was wrong? That would have meant I'd get no other work done. And it really was very important to determine whether he could give me valid information on the theft of the two pedalos—'

'Are you in your right mind?'

'I think so, señor.'

'There are many who would disagree. Why in the name of unreason are you talking about pedalos?'

'To explain why it was necessary to go into the Club.'

'Have I mentioned any club?'

'Not directly, señor. But indirectly—'

'Talking to you, Alvarez, proves that there are those for whom conversation leads to misunderstanding, not understanding. I am not interested in pedalos or any club; I am asking you why you disobeyed orders.'

Not the visit to Club Llueso. Then had Salas somehow learned that he hadn't even started a crime diary? 'As it is Monday—'

55

'You think I need to be told what day of the week it is?'

'It's in rather rough form because often there has been so little time in which to enter the details and so I thought it best to make a fair copy which will take a little time—'

'Have you been drinking?'

'On duty? Of course not, señor.'

'Then are you on drugs?'

'Why should you think that even possible?'

'Because you are talking gibberish.'

'Señor, I'm trying to explain why my crime diary won't be in the post in time to meet the deadline your secretary gave me.'

'Have I mentioned your crime diary?'

'I thought that's what you were questioning.'

'It would help if you didn't jump to conclusions since they are invariably incorrect. I will ask once more.' His voice rose. 'Why have you blatantly disobeyed orders?'

Nothing to do with the Club and not the crime diary. Alvarez spoke with confidence. 'To the best of my belief, señor, I have carefully observed all orders since these are so obviously at the very heart of doing a good job.'

'Where is Exchau Valley?'

'Between here and Laraix, to the east of—'

'You imagine I don't know that?'

Then why ask? He stared at the shuttered window as he wondered if the superior chief had been drinking or was on drugs.

'In whose area is the valley?'

'Inspector Fuster's.'

'You do acknowledge that the valley lies within his authority?'

'Of course, señor.'

'Then will you explain why you've disobeyed orders

56

by carrying out inquiries there without prior reference to him?'

Alvarez had never taken a cold shower in the height of winter, but had little doubt that the shock he suffered now could be compared to the shock that would follow such a stupidity.

'I'm waiting for an answer.'

'Are you referring to my visit to Miguel Munar?'

'Have you made so many inquiries within Inspector Fuster's territory that I need to identify the one I'm referring to?'

'But I have never carried out an inquiry in Exchau Valley.'

'Then Munar is lying when he told the sargento who questioned him that Inspector Alvarez, from Llueso, had assured him he is innocent of smuggling?'

To devote oneself to serving others might preserve a seat in heaven, but it could make for an uncomfortable sprawl on earth. 'All I said to him was—'

'You admit you spoke to Munar about the smuggling?'

'In a sense, yes, but—'

'Then you carried out an inquiry.'

'No, señor. I had a word with Munar as a relation, not a member of the Cuerpo. I explained that all he should, or could, do was tell the truth to the Guardia officers.'

'You did not drive to the head of the valley and question someone else?'

'Well, as a matter of fact I did have a very quick word with the man who works at the house there.'

'And the following day, did you question Señor and Señora Lodge who live in Almerich Valley?'

'I might have had a word with them . . .'

'Inspector Fuster, an officer of the highest calibre, disbelieved Munar, but naturally accepted that the so-called

alibi had to be tested. In consequence, he spoke to Señora
Lodge who referred to the crude, insensitive, and intrusive
questioning to which you had subjected her. Very reluctantly, Inspector Fuster mentioned to me that you had
carried out an investigation within his territory without
any reference to him – very reluctantly, because he dislikes casting the slightest aspersion on a fellow member
of the Cuerpo; but, as he said to me, regretfully there
are times and circumstances when duty must overcome
wishes.'

There was a brief silence.

'Have you the slightest excuse for this blatant breach of
the standing rules of procedure?'

'Señor, I was not carrying out an investigation, I was
trying to help a relative.'

'Any relative of yours would have learned not to ask for
your assistance since that must lead to disaster.' Salas cut
the connexion.

It was a true Monday.

They had just finished the meal when Juan said: 'Uncle
Enrique looks like he's been hit in the cojones!'

Dolores drew in her breath with an audible hiss. 'How
dare you!'

'But—'

'That I should hear my son shame me! Ayee! A wife and
a mother must suffer until the day she dies. Not that all the
blame can be placed on your shoulders. When you have a
father who often talks like a drunken Andaluce, it is to be
expected that occasionally you will do the same.'

'That's not right,' Jaime complained.

'After all you have drunk this meal, you are even less
capable of knowing what is right and what is wrong.'

He murmured something.

'What's that?'

He didn't answer.

She spoke to Juan. 'Up to your bedroom.'

'Why?'

'To learn to clean your mouth out.'

Isabel giggled.

'And you, young lady, up to your bedroom until I tell you to leave it.'

'What for?'

'To learn not to laugh at another's stupidity.'

'It's all Juan's fault.'

'When you are older, you will understand it is invariably a man's fault . . . Upstairs, both of you.'

They stood and slowly made their way up the stairs, as noisily as they dared.

She spoke to her husband. 'Have you retained sufficient senses even to begin to appreciate how your appalling example affects your children?'

'When do I talk like Juan did?' Jaime demanded.

'On the few occasions you manage to restrain your language.' She stood. 'You can put the bottles in the sideboard.'

'I haven't had an after-meal drink yet.'

'Then perhaps you will not drop too many things when you clear the table.'

'Do what?'

'Clear the table, since neither Isabel nor Juan is here to help.'

'And whose fault is that?'

'Yours.' She stared at Alvarez. 'It is true that you have hardly spoken during the meal and you look troubled. Are you ill?'

'Salas has been giving me hell over the phone,' Alvarez answered.

'Why?'

'Because I helped Miguel.' This was his chance to make her appreciate her major part in his misfortune. 'You remember me saying what could happen if I spoke to Miguel as you kept wanting me to do?'

'No.'

'You must.'

'You wish to tell me what I do and don't remember?'

'But I carefully explained that the Guardia might well ask the Cuerpo for help and the next thing, Inspector Fuster would claim I'd been carrying out an inquiry in his area and he'd complain to Salas. And that's precisely what happened.'

'Had you mentioned such a possibility, I would never have suggested you spoke to Miguel.'

He was shocked by the brazenness of the lie.

'Why didn't you explain that Miguel is your cousin?' she asked.

'He isn't, but that's roughly what I said. Salas doesn't accept that makes any difference.'

'How can so stupid a man, even if a Madrileño, be placed in charge of the Cuerpo?'

'That is a question that probably will never be answered.'

'What are you going to do?'

'There's nothing I can do.'

'How like a man to knuckle under at the first sign of trouble!'

'Facts are facts. I made inquiries in another inspector's territory without advising him and that breaks one of the fundamental rules of procedure. In the old days, I expect it was good for a beheading.'

'And now?'

'God knows! . . . But so will I when Salas decides what action to take.'

'There has to be something you can do.'

'I can't think of anything.'

'Would a small coñac help your thoughts?'

Jaime reached for the bottle.

'There is no need for you to drink any more,' she snapped. 'Your problems all stem from yourself.'

Alvarez poured himself a drink, watched by Jaime. As he lifted his glass, the telephone rang. Deciding that for once it would be a good idea to volunteer to answer it, he put the glass down, stood, went through to the front room.

The duty cabo told him that a body, missing head and hands, had been discovered in the mountains. 'Where exactly?'

The answer left no room for doubt: the corpse lay within his territory. Once a Monday, always a Monday.

Seven

A lvarez shivered despite the heat. It was an unwelcome reminder of his mortality to have to look down on a naked, headless male corpse; a reminder made all the starker by the rugged beauty of the setting – mountains to the east and west and between them an uneven floor of rocks, trees, and bushy undergrowth which perfumed the air with the scent of wild herbs.

The doctor, licensed to do police work, crossed to where he stood. 'There's little I can tell you that isn't all too obvious.'

'Can you suggest a time of death?'

'In the heat we've been suffering and in the full sunshine for at least part of the day? . . . Could be anything between two and four weeks. I doubt it's longer than that.'

'There's no wound to the torso?'

'None readily visible, so it's reasonable at this stage to say that the fatal injury was to the head. Which you're going to have to find.'

Since head and hands must have been removed to prevent identification, logically they would have been disposed of well away from the corpse. Nevertheless, the immediate area would have to be thoroughly searched and that would be a gruelling task that would tax even the fittest man. It would best be left to others to carry out.

The doctor used a handkerchief to mop the sweat from

his face and neck. 'Are there any reports of a missing man?'

'None that I've seen.'

'Perhaps this murder reflects trouble amongst the drug dealers?'

'If so, would anyone take such pains to hide the identity of the victim?'

They watched a butterfly zig-zag across several wild sage bushes and then alight on the corpse.

'The dichotomy of existence,' said the doctor, pointing. 'The beautiful vibrancy of life and the ugly stillness of death. Sad to think that beauty can only exist for a fraction of time before it joins the ugly stillness.'

All the scene had lacked until then, Alvarez thought, was a doctor philosophizing on existence.

'There's nothing more I can do, so I'll get back to the village and patients who expect miracles from a mere mortal.' He nodded a goodbye, climbed the sloping, rock-covered ground to the road, some fifty metres higher.

When a doctor admitted he was not omnipotent, a man must whimper . . . Alvarez's mind wandered. That brief pain at the back of his calf when he'd got out of bed – a thrombosis that would defy all cures; that twinge in his chest at the end of the last meal – the harbinger of angina?

A middle-aged man, two cameras slung around his neck, walked up. 'I've taken every photograph I can think of. So I'll move on.'

'OK.'

A cicada started shrilling, to be joined by several more; then all suddenly stopped.

There was the tinkle of sheep bells, but only briefly – since the nearest cultivated land was hundreds of metres away, there must have been a temporary movement of air to bring him the sound, yet not a breath of wind was apparent.

He moved back into the shade of a pine tree, but gained little relief from the heat.

Some ten minutes later, three men, one of them carrying a rolled-up body bag, climbed carefully down to where he stood. One of them moved to view the corpse, whistled. 'Someone didn't like him!'

They rolled the body into the bag, zipped that shut. 'We're a man short,' one of them said as he straightened up, 'so how about giving us a hand to carry this up to the hearse?'

'I've got to stay here and examine the surrounding land.'

'Don't strain yourself, will you?'

He wouldn't. A weak heart must not be stressed. He watched them lift the bag and make a slow, sometimes awkward ascent because the slope became steep and stones and small rocks made footing insecure. They passed out of sight behind a clump of pine trees and thick undergrowth; a moment later, there was the sound of a car's engine starting and of the car driving away.

An attempt had been made to conceal identity; unless the head and hands were found, it might succeed. Corpses could be identified by various means – teeth, for example – but for success there almost always had to be some initial indication as to who the victim might be. There had been no recent reports of a missing man, either an islander or a tourist.

He slowly climbed up to the road, pausing frequently to regain his breath. He would, he promised himself, regain physical well-being – and distance himself from thromboses and heart problems – by smoking less, drinking less, and taking regular exercise.

As he leaned against the car for support, he stared down in the direction of where he had been. A good place to hide the corpse. In one direction, the road swung round and out of sight within two hundred metres, in the other, within a hundred; pine trees, with heavy undergrowth, provided good cover. Whoever had hidden the body must have thought it would either never be discovered or else only after it had degenerated into a skeleton. So how had it come to be found?

Eventually, Alvarez identified who had been on duty at the post. 'Who reported the body?' he asked.

'The name's in the logbook,' the middle-aged cabo replied, a man for whom retirement could not come quickly enough.

'I couldn't find that when I looked for it.'

The cabo scratched his neck. 'I remember. The sargento wanted it for some reason.'

'Then will you tell him I need it.'

'You need it, you tell him.'

Alvarez returned to his room, sat, used the internal phone to speak to the sargento, who tried, by much repeated argument, to avoid having to bring up the logbook. When he finally arrived, he slammed open the door of Alvarez's room, dropped the book on top of the pile of papers and files on the desk. 'This place looks like the bloke who used to work here is dead.' He stamped his way out, slammed the door shut behind himself.

Alvarez yawned. It was small wonder he felt exhausted – the finding of the body had prevented his having a siesta. He opened the logbook. The last entry noted Manuel Jofre had reported the finding of a headless corpse; he had given both his home address and ID number (without which no happening, not even death, was acceptable).

He yawned again. Palma would have to be informed, but since Salas demanded that every report was complete, first Jofre must be questioned to learn the details of his finding of the corpse. What else must be done? He closed his eyes the better to concentrate.

*　　*　　*

The house was in the oldest part of the village, on a rising road so narrow that in the old days even mule carts had found progress difficult; now, cars were forbidden to park in it, but every day they did. As Alvarez walked slowly up the road, he promised himself the pleasure of finding who was the owner of the Peugeot 309, which had prevented his driving into the road and parking, and persuading a member of the Police Local – there was one who owed him a favour – to slap a traffic fine on the owner.

He reached No. 42, stepped through the bead curtain into the relative coolness which came from thick outside rock walls. He called out. A middle-aged woman, dressed in black, entered and he introduced himself, asked if Manuel were her husband?

'My son. Pablo died two years ago.'

'I'm sorry,' he said formally.

'Came back from work and sat in a chair, said he wasn't feeling very well and I went to make him some coffee and when I returned, he was gone. Life becomes death so quick. Father Diego told me it was God's blessing that Pablo had died without suffering. I asked him, where was the blessing for me since I was left on my own when we should have had many more years together? Manuel is a good boy, but sons never help as daughters do. He only returns here to eat and sleep . . .'

He listened patiently; thought how significant it was that women were forever complaining about men whilst men seldom complained about women. She finally became silent. 'I need to have a word with Manuel about what happened earlier.'

'Finding that body upset him something terrible.'

'That's hardly surprising.'

'Rosalía had hysterics.'

'Who's she?'

She was Manuel's novia. Chaste and so unlike some of the girls she could name, but wouldn't. When Rosalía stood before the altar to be married, she'd be able to look up, not down, as most girls should if they possessed an ounce of shame, which they didn't.

He agreed that it was good to know there were still those who honoured virtue. He asked if she could tell him where Manuel was?

Manuel had said nothing when he'd left home, but for certain he would be either at Rosalía's house or Marcos's. Marcos was his great friend and when either of them was in trouble – not, of course, that they were ever in the kind of trouble that would interest the inspector – he turned to the other for comfort. Manuel had been so upset at finding the body and at Rosalía's hysterics . . .

Alvarez left, walked down to his car, drove across the village to a block of recently built flats which offered a standard of comfort unknown in the days when a refrigerator had been a luxury, not a necessity.

Rosalía, her mother told him, was asleep, having been given a sedative by the doctor. The world had become a frightening place – why did he allow such things to happen? To stumble upon a man who had had his head and hands cut off! Was it any wonder that Rosalía was in such a state of shock? She should never have gone for a drive with Manuel. She'd told him so when he'd brought Rosalía back, weeping, shocked . . .

As he took the lift down to the ground floor, Alvarez wondered whether Rosalía's mother's indignation concealed a question she did not want to ask herself – why had the two parked in the middle of nowhere and walked down the rough, sloping land to somewhere even more remote?

He crossed back through the village to a road that skirted both the hill on which much of Llueso stood and the torrente, now a stony gulch, occasionally in winter a raging flood of water; half a kilometre along was a house, standing above the road and built so close to the hill that the rock face was only two metres away from its south side. Both Manuel and Marcos were there. He said he wanted to speak to Manuel on his own and was shown into a small sitting-room, in which, typically, was a television set with a screen far too large for the viewing area – since poverty could still be remembered by many, no chance was missed to show it no longer existed.

Manuel had the sleek looks once termed caddish and he dressed well at his mother's expense. Normally cockily self-assured, for once he was nervous and uncertain.

'God, it was awful!' he said, his voice shaking. 'I keep seeing it in my mind and every time I do . . .'

Life, Alvarez thought, had become too easy for the modern generation; it didn't do them any harm to suffer the need to rediscover the fibre to face the unwelcome. 'Tell me how you discovered the body.'

'I don't want to talk about it.'

'You're going to have to.'

'It makes me feel sick.'

'Swallow hard.'

Manuel looked at Alvarez with uneasy resentment.

'Why did you stop where you did?'

There was no answer.

'On your way down from the road, did you notice anything unusual?'

'I don't know what you mean.'

He explained. Had anything caught their attention (however unlikely in the circumstances)? For instance, a piece of sacking or cloth, caught up on a bramble; marks on

the ground that might suggest something had been dragged
across it?

'We didn't notice anything.'

Love was blind; lust was blinder. 'Who first saw the
body?'

Rosalía had stopped so suddenly his hand . . . She'd
stopped very suddenly. What was that on their right? He'd
said it looked like a foot sticking out beyond the bushes; he'd
been joking. Then, and he would never forget, they'd moved
a little closer and discovered it really was a foot; the foot of
a man who'd had his head and hands hacked off . . .

'Did you touch the body?'

The suggestion horrified Manuel.

Fifteen minutes later, Alvarez left, having learned little
more than that Manuel's mother was almost certainly mistaken; Rosalía might well look up when at the altar, but she
would not have the right to do so.

In his usual parking area near the old square were six hire
cars, leaving no space for his. Tourists! The source of much
prosperity and much resentment. By the time he reached his
office, having had to walk from several roads away, he was
so breathless it was a quarter of an hour before he could
ring Palma.

'Yes?' said the plum-voiced secretary.

'Inspector Alvarez here. I'd like a word with the superior
chief.'

He waited, happy he would be presenting a fully rounded
report which Salas would be unable to criticize. He would
make it clear that a large number of people would be needed
to carry out the search for the head and hands and would
suggest that he should co-ordinate rather than take physical
part . . .

'Yes?' said Salas.

'Señor, I have to report . . .'

'On the principle of better late than never?'

'I don't understand.'

'You tempt me to use that modern vulgarism, "So what's new?"'

'Señor, it's not been possible for me to make a report before now.'

'Should the world come to an end, it will, no doubt, take you a couple of days to realize that fact.'

Would days still exist? 'Earlier, a couple—'

'Found a corpse whose head and hands had been removed.'

'How . . . how did you know that?'

'It has taken you many hours to inform me of the fact. Even for you, that signifies an unusual degree of incompetence.'

'Señor, I had to make preliminary inquiries and those took time.'

'Time for you is elastic and always stretched.'

'But—'

'Are you going to deliver a report?'

'Earlier today, a couple stopped their car on the Laraix road and decided to go for a walk—'

'I understand that the land at that point is very rocky, covered with trees and thick undergrowth, and in parts nearly precipitous. You can believe someone will go for a walk in such hostile surroundings?'

'No, señor.'

'Then why the devil say so?'

'Their intention almost certainly was not to walk, but to find somewhere right out of sight where they could—' He stopped.

'Could what?'

'You know.'

'Would I ask if I did?'

'Make love.'

There was a long silence. Then Salas said: 'Whenever I am in danger of forgetting that your mind has a sewer-like quality, you are at pains to remind me of that fact.'

'When a couple go to such lengths to find a private spot—'

'You are unable to accept they may be doing something as blameless as enjoying a walk?'

The hypocrisy of that comment – only a moment before, Salas had, by inference, derided the possibility – was too great to be ignored. 'As you have just pointed out, when the land is so hostile, who would ever go there just for the pleasure of walking?'

Salas ignored the question. 'Did you call the police doctor to the scene?'

'Of course.'

'What were his conclusions?'

'He estimates death as having taken place between two and four weeks ago; however, in the heat even that wide spread of time may not be sufficient.'

'Doctors rush to cover their mistakes even before they make them.'

Such forethought was not unknown in other professions. 'As yet, there's nothing to challenge the assumption the man was killed where he was found. Obviously, head and hands were removed in order to prevent identification and unless we find these, may succeed. Without identification, there can be little hope of solving the crime. So what I propose is that I organize a search of the area. Whilst it would seem logical for the murderer to dispose of the head and hands as far from the body as possible, logic often gets forgotten because of emotional stress . . .'

'A search will require a great number of people and offer little chance of success.'

'Yet unless and until we can identify the victim—'

'His name is Felipe Marti.'

'How can you say that, señor?'

'Inspector Fuster informed me earlier that that was almost certainly the dead man's name. When it became clear I had no idea what he was talking about, he appeared very surprised I had not been kept fully informed of events. Since you were in charge of the case, I doubt his expressed surprise was genuine.'

'He must have been working in my territory, yet he has never contacted me and asked—'

'To accuse from ignorance is to betray one's lack of character. Inspector Fuster scrupulously observes all procedural rules.'

'Then how come he knows anything about the case?'

'He learned about it from someone who had spoken to a relative who works for the doctor in Llueso who was called to examine the corpse. It is quite possible that someone else would – since it was not his case – have done nothing on receipt of this information. However, Inspector Fuster is a dedicated officer. He asked himself if he knew of anyone who had recently disappeared in circumstances that could suggest he had been murdered. The name of Marti immediately came to mind. Fifteen days ago, a young man—'

'How young?'

'Don't interrupt.'

'But—'

'Fifteen days ago, Marti disappeared from his home in Canyois and since then his family has had no word from him.'

'Can anyone suggest why he hasn't returned home?'

'Being murdered is not reason enough?'

'To put it another way, is there any suggestion why he should have been murdered?'

'As Inspector Fuster told me – in discreet terms, very

different from those you are accustomed to use – he has ascertained that Marti and another man were very friendly with a woman whose reputation does not flatter her. Inspector Fuster suggests that the emotions of the two men became so antagonistically involved that one murdered the other.'

'That seems a bit far-fetched when one realizes that if it was so well known they were both after the same bit of crumpet—'

'Would that you could show even a tithe of Inspector Fuster's sense of discretion!'

'. . . that they were both friendly with her. If one of them was murdered, the other would automatically become prime suspect; in such circumstances, an attempt to conceal the identity of the corpse by dramatic means would not only be futile, it would underline guilt.'

'A villager is incapable of such constructive thought.'

'Another thing. I asked what was meant by "young man" because from the look of the corpse, the victim was much more middle-aged than young.'

'Are you a forensic anatomist?'

'No, señor.'

'Then leave such judgments to someone who is. It is certain that since people of small intelligence revel in sordid matters, the inhabitants of this island will follow the course of this case with morbid interest. It must, therefore, be solved quickly. To ensure this, I intend to use the authority vested in me to appoint Inspector Fuster to head the investigation as soon as he can organize himself to take charge.'

'You can't do that. It's my area,' Alvarez protested.

'For reasons just given, there must be no risk of this case becoming so confused that solution is impossible. You will work with Inspector Fuster and I suggest you pay close attention to the way in which he carries out his duties – there has to be the possibility you will benefit from learning how things should be done.' Salas cut the connexion.

Alvarez stared at the far wall. Work under that little shite? Sooner resign. Face Salas and say, 'Either I'm in charge of the case or I quit the Cuerpo.' He slowly replaced the receiver. It was all too easy to judge Salas's reaction to such a threat. 'Sign here.'

If he could have foreseen the future, he would have lived off half-cooked chick peas in tasteless sauce for weeks rather than speak to Miguel about the accusation of smuggling.

Eight

Fuster spoke occasionally with a slight lisp because he believed this to be the mark of an aristocratic background; when he looked in a mirror, he saw Adonis; he was untroubled by intellectual modesty. He stood in the centre of the room and in a tone of distaste said: 'This room is in a mess.'

'I've been too busy to bother about tidying up—'Alvarez began.

'I'd like you to clear everything.'

'Why?'

'Because I cannot work when surrounded by muddle.'

'Are you thinking of sharing this room?'

'No. It will be mine from now on.'

'You can forget that idea for a start.'

'If you object, raise the matter with the superior chief. But you may as well know now that he assured me I have complete overall authority.'

So ten to one, there was only frustration to be gained from appealing to Salas. When a wise man came to a dangerously steep cliff, he either tried to find a way round it or remained where he was. 'I'll arrange things,' he said wearily.

'I'll give you your orders when I've studied what has already been done. If anything has.'

'I need to go down to the port because I've two cases there – minor ones, but—'

'They must wait.'

Alvarez crossed to the door, telling himself that if the little runt was determined to make a fool of himself, so be it. He gripped the handle. Yet it went against the grain to watch someone walk towards an open pozo negro and not warn him. He let go of the handle. 'The superior chief said you thought the dead man might well be Felipe Marti.'

'Yes.'

'How old is Marti?'

'Twenty-four.'

'Have you seen the body of the dead man?'

'No. Nor have I seen any photographs of the scene of the crime. I suppose you had some taken?' Fuster asked doubtfully.

'They're being developed. I'd judge the body was that of a man several years older than twenty-four.'

'Really?'

'Yes.'

'Interesting. Get this desk cleared as soon as possible and whilst you're about it, clean the floor.'

'There's a daily woman who does that sort of thing.'

'Obviously, very occasionally.'

Alvarez opened the door and left.

'You're looking gloomier than ever,' the bartender in Club Llueso said, as he passed a glass of brandy across the counter. 'So what's the problem – a woman?'

'If only it were that simple.'

'You think women are simple? You've got a real problem.'

'I've got a self-satisfied, ignorant, concrete-headed twit giving the orders.'

'You've moved into politics?'

'A fellow inspector has been detailed to take over my case.'

'So why the gloom? Saves you the bother of having to try to cope, surely?'

'D'you know,' Alvarez said, slowly and disbelievingly, 'I hadn't looked at things in that light before. I must be getting very old. And I'm betting the case won't be nearly as simple as he reckons and before long he'll be wishing he'd stayed in Santa Amelia.'

'My uncle used to say that the villagers from there were so dim, they swore the earth was flat.'

'I'll have another coñac to drink to your uncle.'

Alvarez's newly found cheerfulness survived only until his return to the post. About to walk past the duty desk, the cabo stopped him. 'Enrique, that new inspector's been shouting for you.'

'Have you any idea why?'

'I don't reckon it's to pin a medal on you. Not after I told him you were in the Club, having a liquid merienda.'

Alvarez's voice rose. 'You what?'

The cabo laughed. 'There's no call for panic. What I really said was that you were out on a case.'

'One of these days, your sense of humour is going to give someone heart failure.'

He walked on, climbed the stairs, paused to regain his breath, and then, without thinking, entered his old room.

Fuster sat behind the desk. 'I've been trying to contact you for the past twenty minutes,' he observed curtly.

'I had to go out on a job.'

'In future you will leave word before you do that. Which reminds me, I haven't yet seen your crime diary.'

'It's at home so that I can make out a fair copy in my spare time.'

'You will keep it here from now on and make certain

every relevant aspect of this murder case is recorded . . .
Tell me, have you been drinking?'

'No.'

'There seems to be a slight smell of coñac.'

'If I'd been drinking, there'd be a strong smell.'

Fuster hesitated, then said: 'You're to drive over to
Canyois now and find out what anyone can tell you about
relations between Marti and Vich.'

'Who's Vich?'

'The second man who's friendly with Teresa Llabres. Do
you need to be told who she is?'

'I can probably guess.'

'In particular, has anyone overheard Vich threatening
Marti with physical harm.'

Alvarez left and made his way downstairs.

'Did you grovel?' the duty cabo asked.

'Just told him what he could do to himself.'

'If I believed you, I'd buy you the biggest drink you've
ever had.'

Canyois was a typical inland village. Originally sited on a
hill for defensive purposes, it had begun to expand many
years before and now spread out across the surrounding
land. Houses in the old part were side by side; houses
and bungalows in the newer areas were detached and set
in gardens – rising prosperity had allowed the people to
enjoy personal space and relative quiet.

After calling at a bar for information where he bought a
brandy purely as a gesture of goodwill, he parked in the
small square where once the paseo – circles of young men
and young women who walked slowly around in opposite
directions, their minds filled with questions which nearby
elderly relatives were determined should not be answered
until a priest's blessing had been given – had been a feature

of village life. He left the car and slowly climbed the narrow Calle Reina Constanza – passing a traditional corner shop that had so far survived the onslaught of the supermarkets – to No. 7.

He stepped through the bead curtain and called out. Almost immediately, a woman entered the front room through the far doorway. Young, but perhaps not as young as she tried to make out, she was attractive in the style that a prude would term, very obvious. A September plum, filled with the warmth and sweetness of a long, hot summer, was his grandiloquent description. 'Señorita Teresa Llabres?'

'Well?'

'My name is Inspector Alvarez . . .'

'Another one!'

'I believe Inspector Fuster has had a word with you?'

'And not many more because I told the little forastero pisspot to clear off.'

Spirited as well as ripe.

'So what do you want?'

'I'd like a chat.'

'And if I wouldn't?'

'Then I'll have come a long way to no purpose.' He smiled. He told her he hoped very much she'd help him because Inspector Fuster had made such a cock-up of everything – as forasteros usually did – that he was now trying to sort things out. He projected himself as a warm-hearted character, seldom judging because life had taught him circumstances could make white black in the blink of an eyelid.

She became far more friendly and offered him a drink. They went through to the back room. When she handed him a brandy, with ice, she leaned forward and her décolletage widened; when she sat, her short skirt rode well up her thighs. Experience told him she would not have missed his interest, so did her lack of reserve mean . . . ? He was a fool. A woman of her age would treat any advance from him with amusement; nothing reduced a man so quickly as laughter. 'Obviously, what's brought me here is that Felipe seems to have disappeared.'

'That little pisspot tried to say he's dead.' She spoke with bitter sarcasm. 'He thinks there was a row between him and Carlos.'

'And there wasn't one?'

'They are always arguing because of me.' She spoke with pride.

'Hardly surprising.'

The inferred flattery pleased her. Unasked, she explained the relationships. The three of them were always together – except, that was, when really it was not a very good idea. She looked at him out of the corner of her eye and he nodded to show he understood what she meant.

She thought of them as friends and rivals. Friends when they were all together, rivals when they were not. Let a man see himself as a rival and he became a more attentive, and better, lover. Didn't he agree? He agreed. But, he asked, had the two men ever let this rivalry lead to real trouble between them? Of course not. Not even when Carlos had been unable to go to The Festival of Sex in Barcelona that people had said was so amusing. Did he think sex was amusing? Desirably so. 'I'll bet that little pisspot wouldn't say the same!'

'He'd make it illegal.'

They'd arranged everything before Carlos had suddenly been unable to leave with them. He'd begged them to wait three days, but Felipe had laughed and said that now the trip was going to be even more amusing. Carlos had threatened to cut off Felipe's pelotas so that the trip became a disaster, but that was only a joke. And because she believed in fairness, when she and Felipe had returned from Barcelona, she'd spent three nights with Carlos. That had annoyed Felipe, but afterwards everything had been as before.

'You don't think Carlos in reality had not been reconciled to your trip to Barcelona and he killed Felipe out of jealousy?'

'Jealous of what?'

'That you spent time with Felipe.'

'That made it all the more exciting for Carlos when he was with me.'

'Nevertheless, Felipe has disappeared and his family don't know where he is.'

'Because he hasn't told them.'

'Why wouldn't he?'

'Because they call me what I am not.'

'Have you any idea where Felipe is now?'

'Of course I know.'

'Where is he?'

'On the Peninsula.'

'What's he doing there?'

'Looking for jobs for the three of us so we can leave the island and his parents, whose tongues are covered in thorns. When we've moved, we can really enjoy ourselves.'

'I rather gathered that's what you've been doing.'

'Here, one can't really let go. People are such prudes.'

'Can you be certain he is on the Peninsula?'

'What stupid questions you ask.'

'That's because I am a stupid person.'

'I like you; you couldn't be more different from that little pisspot. Have another drink?'

When she handed him the refilled glass, she leaned forward even further than before; when she sat, her skirt rode higher – or was this, honesty compelled him to ask himself, optimistic imagination? 'Felipe has been keeping in touch with you?'

'Every evening, he phones and demands I deny Carlos since he is working for all of us and therefore Carlos should suffer as much as him. I tell him I am doing just that. He knows I'm lying and becomes so jealous that when he returns—'

'Will he be phoning you this evening?'

'Naturally. And I will tell him I am keeping my promise. And everything will be that little bit more exciting with Carlos because I lied to Felipe. Isn't life wonderful?'

'Sometimes . . . When you've finished lying to him, tell him to go to the nearest Guardia post to identify himself.'

'Why should he bother?'

'Because then I'll be able to make Fuster look a fool.'

'I will tell him to do so or when he returns, he will lead the life of a monk.'

He finished his drink. 'You should have told Fuster all this because it would have saved a great deal of trouble.'

'And I would have done had the little pisspot not spoken with curled lips. In his mind, he was calling me puta. But if I'd said, come back when it's dark and no one can see you enter, he would have come running. I hate men who hide themselves.'

He stood. She hoped they'd meet again. As he walked carefully down the steep road to the square, he wondered how she'd react if he returned when it was dark? As he settled behind the wheel of his car, he swore. Did other men suffer the frustration of believing the impossible might be possible? The truth was as stark as it was simple. In the eyes of a young, ripe woman, only a fortune could strip the years from a man who had been maturing a little too long.

Nine

W hen Alvarez stepped into his old room, it was as if he were entering new territory. The top of the desk was bare, the chair with a broken leg had been replaced by an undamaged one, the small bookcase contained a neat row of text books instead of a collapsed pile of paperbacks and magazines, the last year's calendar featuring a lady of obvious charms had vanished, and there was a carpet on the floor. Since Fuster was not there, he turned to leave; at that moment, the other hurried through the doorway.

Fuster passed him, went round the desk, and sat. 'You've been away longer than I expected.'

'I've been talking to Teresa Llabres.'

'And others?'

'No.'

'It's somewhat surprising you should have seen fit to spend so much time with her.'

'Perhaps I got more out of her than she was willing to give you.'

The set of Fuster's lips showed he chose to find ambiguity in the words. 'It did not occur to you to question others?'

'No.'

'Why not?'

'Where's the point?'

'I need to explain even that?'

'Marti is on the Peninsula, searching for jobs for himself,

Teresa, and Vich because they want to get away from the island.'

'Teresa told you that?

'Yes.'

'If it were true, she would have told me when I questioned her.'

'Not necessarily. She said you were rudely abrupt, which so annoyed her she decided to tell you nothing.'

'Ridiculous!'

'It can happen with us Mallorquins when we gain the impression that someone from a big city is looking down on us.'

'If I find that what you claim is fact, I shall consider charging her with an attempt to pervert the course of justice.'

'Not very advisable. Do that and it's odds on she'll claim you're hounding her in revenge.'

'Revenge for what?'

'Refusing to bed you after dark.'

'Are you out of your mind?'

'From jealousy? Hardly.'

Fuster's expression suggested his thoughts were rather emotional for a man who prided himself on his self-control. Finally, he said: 'Can she prove what she claims?'

'That you tried to set up an assignation?'

'No!' he shouted. He brought a handkerchief out of his trouser pocket and mopped his face. 'The superior chief is far too generous,' he muttered. He returned the handkerchief to his trouser pocket. 'Can she prove Marti is on the Peninsula?'

'Marti rings her every evening so I've said to tell him to report to the nearest Guardia post and identify himself. When we receive confirmation he's done that, we'll know he's not the victim you've been so certain he is.'

Fuster was about to speak, then checked the words. He

tapped on the desk with the fingers of his right hand. He cleared his throat. 'As I have made very clear from the beginning, it was possible, but no more than that, Marti was the victim.'

'As Lopez wrote, nothing so deflects criticism as a convenient memory.'

'What are you suggesting?'

'That Lopez had been around.'

Fuster stopped tapping with his fingers and withdrew his hand. 'I find your attitude objectionable.'

'And here was I, beginning to think I wasn't making an impression.'

There was a long silence which Alvarez broke. 'Assuming Marti proves he is still alive, presumably we'll have to organize a search for the head and hands?'

Fuster spoke in clipped, angry tones, with no trace of a lisp. 'Because of the labour this would involve, that is a decision the superior chief will make.'

'Do we in the meantime contact hotels, aparthotels, hostals, travel agents, and car hire firms, to find out if they know of someone who's gone missing?'

Fuster picked up a pencil and tapped one end up and down on the palm of his hand. 'You've rung Forensic to find out if they can give us any information?'

'No. You're the man who gives the orders.'

'I've been making the mistake of presuming you'll show a slight degree of initiative. Ask them.'

Alvarez turned.

'And prepare a time correlation chart, a statement time-check chart, and a statement and information cross-check chart.'

As he walked along the corridor to the small, stuffy room which was now his, he wondered what Fuster had been talking about.

He slumped down in the chair. Fuster was not going to disappear until the case was solved, therefore this had to be achieved as quickly as humanly possible. He jerked himself upright, lifted the receiver, dialled the number.

An assistant at the Institute for Forensic Anatomy said Professor Fortunato was away at a meeting; however, he could provide a provisional finding in the case of the headless man. The victim was a male Caucasian, aged somewhere between thirty-five and forty-five. Height, one metre seventy-seven. Build, slight, physical condition reasonable, but not good – he was not a manual worker. No signs of recent injury. Several years previously, he had suffered a severe fracture of the fibula shaft of the left leg which had most probably left him with a marked limp. Death about three weeks ago.

'Not much practical help in identifying him, I'd guess?'

'I can't see that it is at the moment.'

'Keep at it and one day you'll find out who he was and why someone so disliked him.'

One could cheerfully forecast success when one did not have to bear the consequences of failure.

Dolores helped herself to a plateful of Sopas Mallorquinas, then sat. 'Cousin Luisa rang earlier.'

Alvarez braced himself.

'She says the sargento has not returned for a few days and the last time he was at Ca'n Portens he was not so aggressive. It seems you could be right, Enrique – the best thing was for Miguel to say and do nothing.'

He ate a spoonful of the bread soup with added pleasure.

'It proves there's always a first time,' Jaime said.

'What are you talking about?' she asked.

'Enrique being right.' He chuckled.

86

'One of my mother's favourite sayings was, "Only stupid words come out of empty mouths."'

'Your mother—'

'Yes?'

'She knew a lot of sayings,' he mumbled.

'My mother was a very well-read person,' she said proudly. Few people of her mother's background had been able to read. 'Cousin Luisa also told me Jorge has bought a new Mercedes and Mario is talking about moving into an even bigger home. They are two sons to be proud of.'

'How do they make so much money?' Jaime asked with jealous curiosity.

'By working,' she snapped.

Far more likely, Alvarez thought, that almost all Miguel's profits from smuggling were passed directly on to them. Miguel and Luisa had known many years of hardship and when their sons had been young could offer them little more than loving care. Now, it gave them immense pleasure and pride to enable their sons to live lives far different from their own; and somehow they managed to blind their minds to the fact that it was this money which had turned their sons into snobs who were ashamed of them.

'Cousin Luisa has asked us to a meal as thanks for helping them.'

'That's fair enough!' Jaime said.

'If she repays your contribution, we'll have only dry bread.'

'I was ready to do all I could.'

'Only when you knew that that was nothing . . . She will ring again to say when the meal will be.'

'I'm not certain if I'll be able to go,' Alvarez said.

'I am.'

'But now Fuster's in charge—'

'Nothing could be ruder than to refuse when she's trying to thank us for what some of us did for her and Miguel.'

'It will be out of my hands.'

'You will take hold of it again.'

Alvarez ate. If only one could manage one's own life as easily as someone else's.

'While I was shopping this morning,' she continued, 'I met Eva. Far too good a woman to suffer that husband of hers who drinks until he accuses her of wishing him dead.'

'Could be he's right,' Jaime muttered.

'What's that?'

'It's just that I've heard—'

'The man who listens to gossip listens to lies.'

'I suppose your mother said that?'

'I say it.'

For a while, they ate in silence.

Women, Alvarez acknowledged as he drove through the village, could seldom, perhaps never, be relied upon. He'd impressed on Dolores the need for him to arrive at the post on time now Fuster was there, yet she had left him to sleep merely because she had called him thrice without effect.

He parked his car and walked, more quickly than he welcomed, the short distance to the post. 'Is Inspector Fuster here?' he asked the duty cabo.

'You sound like you've just run a marathon.'

'That's exactly how I feel . . . Is Fuster here?'

'Went out in a rush twenty minutes ago.'

Twenty minutes ago, he would only have been a few minutes late. Not even Fuster could complain about that. He climbed the stairs and as he drew level with his old room, the phone in there rang. He hesitated, then went in and answered the call. A sargento in Salamanca reported that Felipe Marti had presented and identified himself and given his present address.

Alvarez thanked the other, replaced the receiver and, not thinking about what he was doing, sat. It was only when the lack of muddle on the desk intrigued him, that he came to his senses. He stood and was about to leave when it occurred to him that he had the opportunity to make Salas aware of the fact that Fuster could be very wrong. He sat once more, dialled.

'Yes,' said the secretary with practised curtness.

'Inspector Alvarez here. Can I have a word with the superior chief?'

'Wait.'

He waited.

'What is it?' Salas asked, speaking even more curtly than his secretary had done.

'Señor, I have just had a call from the Guardia in Salamanca to say Felipe Marti has identified himself to them. So he is not dead.'

'It is surprising to hear you be so logical.'

'Despite the points I raised at the time, Inspector Fuster has maintained—'

'Very recently, he said to me that although Marti had disappeared, was known to have had an angry row before his disappearance, and his parents had not heard from him, it would be a mistake to jump to conclusions.'

'That's a very long way from what he's been saying before I found out the truth.'

'It is one of the traits of an efficient police officer that he has the breadth and flexibility of mind to realize that whilst facts can't lie, false conclusions can be drawn from them. You would do well to remember that.'

Normally, Alvarez would never have tried to belittle someone else, but there were limits to any man's sense

of fairness. 'Who was it who originally pointed out that
Marti was in his mid-twenties, but the body appeared to be
that of an older man?'

'Inspector Fuster rightly said that appearances can be
deceptive, yet must never be held to be so until there is
proof that they are.'

'When he took over the case, he insisted the dead man
was Marti, appearances or no appearances. I told him I didn't
think so.'

'To a man of lesser sagacity, that would have been reason
for greater certainty.'

'Who was it persuaded Teresa to tell the truth so that we
learned Marti is alive? She co-operated with me because I
didn't sneer when she told me about enjoying a ménage à
trois—'

'I never cease to be astonished that an officer in the
Cuerpo should take so open an interest in salacious matters.'

'The relationship was important.'

'To someone of a certain mind.'

'The two men could be both rivals and friends; they could
have bitter rows one day and drink together the next; each
could be consumed with jealousy one night, triumphant the
next when—'

'I have heard more than enough. You will inform Inspector Fuster that in future all reports to me are to be made by
him and not by you. He is a man whose moral standard is
beyond reproach. He would not revel, as you do, in speaking
about such matters.'

'In this case, it might well be that that is because it is a
sore point.'

Salas cut the connexion.

Alvarez replaced the receiver. He should have remembered the goat who, seeing his reflection in the water and

thinking he was faced by a rival, charged and drowned. But there was more than one way of picking the fruit of the prickly pear without spearing oneself on the nearly invisible thorns. Salas was unwilling to admit Fuster was an opportunist, ever ready to promote himself at the expense of his colleagues; that unwillingness could be overcome. He, Enrique Alvarez, would ensure this by solving the case.

The body was that of an unknown man, yet there had been no report of a missing person sufficiently recently to be apposite. But, by chance, he knew was that there was one man who had not reappeared as could have been expected. Could that unknown Englishman who had called at Miguel's finca, at the home of the German and, perhaps, at the home of the Perrys, be the dead man? Miguel had mentioned that the man limped. Forensic said the dead man had probably limped. The more he considered the possibility, the more possible it seemed . . . The Englishman (assuming that was his nationality) had arrived at Ca'n Portens in, presumably, a hired car. Therefore, as he'd previously suggested to Dolores (yet taken no steps to implement) all car hire firms should be asked if a car had not been returned at the end of the contract. This Englishman had been searching for someone whom he believed lived in either Exchau or Almerich Valley, so it seemed likely he would have been staying as close to that area as possible. There were few hotels anywhere in the mountains and none within several kilometres of the valleys, so logically he would have based himself in Port Llueso, Cala Roig, or Playa Neuva – hotels, aparthotels, and self-service apartments in those resorts must be contacted and asked if a tourist had gone missing. On the face of things, it might seem that since the police had received no report of an absconding guest, there had not been one. But every year, several tourists left unannounced and without paying their bills – in effect, disappearing – but such frauds were seldom reported to the police because the amounts involved were usually not large enough to warrant the trouble any investigation would cause. Only a shrug of the shoulders might have marked the Englishman's disappearance – why should anyone imagine he could have ended up as the headless, handless corpse found many days later . . . ?

Pursuing the possibility, then, the staff in every hotel, aparthotel, hostal, and self-catering flat in the three coastal resorts must be questioned. But for one man to set out to do that on his own was quixotically absurd.

He stood. Despite the proud promises to himself, common sense said he had to forget the crazy idea of solving the case on his own . . . Yet had he not been thrown out of his own room by that self-satisfied little weasel? Had he not earlier hurried dangerously quickly to the post for fear that his late arrival might be noticed? When next it was merienda time, would he not sneak across to the Club Llueso for fear of going openly and being seen? Was he content to live his future in the shadow of fear and oppression? It was a time to gird up the loins and stiffen the sinews. He slowly sat. Perhaps tomorrow?

Ten

Alvarez walked along the pedestrianized front, passing on his left the tables set outside the bars at which tourists sat and paid twice as much for whatever they ate and drank as they would have done at a bar or café back from the sea; on his right, men, women, and children lazed on the sand or in the bath-warm sea. So blatant a pursuit of leisure made his own activity seem that much more onerous.

He reached the Hotel Platjador, entered the air-conditioned reception area, and crossed to the counter, behind which a young reception clerk, formally dressed, patiently listened as a middle-aged, obese woman complained in strident English about breakfast – no porridge, no eggs and bacon, just two something-or-others (ensaimadas, murmured the clerk), jam that had tasted funny, no marmalade, and the tea had been nothing like the tea she made at home in Liverpool. The clerk promised her he'd have a word with someone.

'Aye, you do that,' were her final words before she walked away, certain she had helped to preserve civilized values.

'Porridge in this heat?' Alvarez said to the reception clerk.

'When you've done this job for a while, nothing surprises.'

'So will you serve it?'

'Of course not.'

'Then won't she be back tomorrow morning, complaining even more loudly?'

'Probably, but since I won't be on duty then, that won't be my problem.'

A reaction Alvarez could appreciate. He explained what he wanted.

'You'd best have a word with the assistant manager. Hang on while I see if he's free.'

A couple of minutes later, Alvarez was called to the end of the counter, the flap was lifted, and he was directed to a doorway beyond the key-board.

The assistant manager – tall, thin, face pale because he was so seldom in the sun – came round the desk and shook hands. 'Not seen you for a long time, Inspector.'

Alvarez couldn't remember a previous meeting, but agreed it was a long time since they had last met.

'Have a seat. And would you care for a coffee?'

'I'd like a cortado, thanks.'

The assistant manager ordered one cortado, one con leche over the internal phone. He replaced the receiver. 'So what brings you here? Nothing to cause us trouble, I hope?'

'It won't keep you awake at nights. Roughly three weeks ago, did you have a guest go missing?'

'Three weeks,' he said reflectively, rubbing his pointed chin with thumb and forefinger.

The inner door opened and a man in white shirt and dark trousers looked in. 'Sorry, didn't know you were busy.'

'That's all right. If the inspector will permit? What is it?'

'Susana reports the handbasin in seventeen is blocked.'

'Has she tried to clear it?'

'Without success. Reckons there's been some sort of gunge shoved down the drain. There were kids in the room, so that's likely enough. The new guest says that if it's not cleared immediately, her husband will get on to the tour operator and tell them the room is not fit for habitation.'

He sighed. 'The day I win the lottery, I'll tell the first complaining guest what I really think . . . Go and see if there's anything you can do. If there isn't, call the plumber and ask him to come immediately. If he can't or won't, we'll have to find the couple another room – maybe forty-one; that's become so noisy, it's not normally being used.'

As the one man left, another arrived with a tray on which were two cups of coffee. The assistant manager passed the smaller cup and saucer across. 'Your cortado . . . Drains block, taps won't run or won't stop running, a drunken party has a sing-song at three in the morning – small wonder that if we've only a couple of ulcers, we count ourselves lucky.'

'If you want to know what real trouble is, join the police,' Alvarez said.

'Then you suffer from so many ulcers, you'll refuse a coñac to go with the coffee?'

'I like living dangerously.'

The assistant manager smiled wryly, swivelled his chair round to open a small cupboard door, brought out a half-full bottle of Soberano and two glasses. 'I keep this for guests who complain more than most. If they're English, the fact they're getting something for free calms them right down, if French, they spend so much time telling me it's not nearly as good as cognac, they forget what they were originally moaning about . . . Help yourself.' He passed a glass and the bottle across.

Alvarez poured himself a good measure.

'Water?'

'Is there any ice?'

'I'll send for some.' He spoke over the internal phone. As he gave himself a small brandy, he said: 'You're asking about a missing guest. We had a couple last week who cleared off without paying their wine bills . . .'

A waiter brought in an ice bucket, at a gesture from the assistant manager passed it to Alvarez, left.

The assistant manager drank some coffee, then some brandy. 'And we had a runner something like three weeks ago. Must say, he didn't seem the type, but you can never really tell. The most apparently honest man I've met took the owner of this hotel for more money than he'd ever admit.'

'Tell me about the runner.'

'I'll have to check to remind myself.' He drank some more coffee, then leaned over and pulled open the bottom drawer of the desk, brought out a file. He shuffled through some papers, read, said: 'Disappeared between the ninth and the tenth. Took us for a little over sixty thousand pesetas.'

'What can you tell me about him?'

'Name of Gates. He booked in on the morning of the seventh for a fortnight. We mostly only have package holidays, but if there's a vacancy and a casual wants a room, naturally we have him in since he's better profit.'

Arriving in the morning, Alvarez thought, allowed plenty of time to be searching for the address by eight that evening. 'You've got his passport details?'

'Of course. You want them?'

'I don't think I need them just yet . . . When did you discover he'd gone?'

The assistant manager again checked through the papers in the file, found the one he wanted, read. 'One of the maids went in to do the room on the tenth – that's the Saturday. The bed hadn't been slept in and she noticed the bathroom had been cleared of all personal items. She checked the bedroom cupboard and chest of drawers and they were all empty, so she told the desk. My opposite number put him down as a professional runner.'

Alvarez's faint optimism vanished. Gates had booked in for a fortnight as a bluff, not because he had intended to stay that long.

'The only other thing I can tell you is he lost his cigarette lighter and said he must have left it in his room. Was very concerned about it, and all but accused the staff of pinching it. We naturally made inquiries, but the maid who cleaned his room swore she'd seen no lighter.'

'Presumably it was a pretty good one or he'd not have made such a fuss?'

'He claimed it was silver and a family gift.' The assistant manager shrugged his shoulders. 'Perhaps he was setting up a scam on an insurance company or a smokescreen for his vanishing act – implanting the idea there was no way he'd be leaving until he got it back. Their kind are good psychologists. I'll bet he spends the summer taking hotel after hotel . . . Have you heard about him from somewhere else?'

'In a way,' Alvarez answered. It never hurt to let the public know the Cuerpo were always on their toes.

'He won't take any one hotel for all that much, but add up all his swindles and they must represent a tidy sum. And let's not forget the hotel owners who reckon their managers and assistant managers should be mind readers and recognize a runner as he arrives, not after he's gone . . . Natalia might be able to tell you a bit more about him than I can.'

'Who's she?'

'The maid who reported he'd skipped.'

There was small point in talking to her, but it would have been churlish to have said so. 'I'll have a word with her.'

'She'll be at home. I'll give you her address.' The assistant manager activated the PC on the desk, tapped several keys. The printer worked briefly. He passed a sheet of paper across.

When, a few minutes later, Alvarez stepped out of the hotel, he was determined to make further inquiries at at least two more hotels. But the heat, made even more oppressive because of the contrast with the cool of the air-conditioning, stripped away all energy and resolution. Faced by so monumental a task, he told himself, it would be common sense not to wear himself out at the very beginning. Much better to take things calmly. Tomorrow would be time enough to resume asking questions . . . He made for his car.

As he stopped at the first set of lights on the Llueso road – still regarded by many motorists as offering advice rather than commands – he began to think he should have checked out at least one more hotel before stopping. If every time he felt hot and tired he packed up work, would the task ever be completed?

The car behind hooted impatiently and he realized the lights had changed to green. He drove forward. Suppose he changed his mind and visited one more hotel? Yet . . . The car behind him hooted again. He turned right. The short road he was in had once ended at green fields; now, there was a T-junction and beyond flats and houses. So many fields were disappearing under concrete. Would there soon be none of the original coastal beauty left – which was what had first attracted visitors? Perhaps natural calamity would strike and tourists would no longer come to the island; hotels, aparthotels, hostals, appartment blocks, discothèques, night clubs, bars, restaurants, and the rest of tourism would crumble into rubble and beauty would return. But with it, would there also come poverty? Life might offer sugar on one side, but there was almost always salt on the other.

He turned right at the T-junction and almost immediately did the same again. A road sign told him he was in Carrer General Ansaldo – the road in which Natalia lived. Since he was there, was there any point in stopping and talking to her? He could think of one. It would leave him with a clear conscience, yet not enough time to question the staff at a second hotel.

No. 7 was one of several side-by-side, one-floor houses, which abutted directly on to the narrow pavement. With shutters closed against the sun, there was an air of bleakness about it that was not dispelled by the two window boxes filled with flowers. It was an erroneous impression. Inside there was considerable comfort and beyond the back door was a small patio in which grew single orange, lemon, and tangerine trees, each one vigorously productive because the land had for years been manured by pigs, before the law – thanks to the susceptibilities of town tourists – had decreed that farm animals were no longer to be kept in villages.

Natalia was in her late twenties. She stood in the centre of the front room and said, 'What's the matter?' with the sharp nervousness of someone who always faced authority with uneasy respect.

He assured her, in his most friendly style, that he only wanted to talk to her about the Englishman . . . He was interrupted by a child's call from the next room. She hurriedly left.

When she returned, she was pushing a pram in which her daughter was now asleep. 'Sorry about that.'

'No call to be.'

She bent over the pram and rearranged the single sheet over her daughter, straightened up. 'Aren't you going to sit?'

He settled on one of the leather armchairs, uncomfortable in the heat, but in vogue.

She moved the pram alongside the second armchair and sat. 'What Englishman are you talking about?'

'His name was Gates and he booked into the hotel for

a fortnight, some three weeks ago, but vanished after only two nights.'

'And upset Lucía—' She stopped, clearly regretting she had spoken.

'Who's Lucía?'

'Same as me; one of the maids.'

'Why did Señor Gates's disappearance upset her?'

'I shouldn't be telling.'

'What I'm told, goes no further – I'm like a priest.'

'I wouldn't say you were like Father Ortiz, what with . . . And I shouldn't be saying that either! Santiago – my husband – says I couldn't keep a secret even if I was paid.'

'That's what my cousin says about me.' It promoted a friendly feeling to suggest one shared another's weaknesses . . . In what way did he differ so markedly from Father Ortiz – to his advantage or the priest's? 'Tell me why Lucía was concerned?'

She spoke hesitantly at first, then more freely. Lucía was older, although she'd never admit that fact. She'd been working at the Hotel Platjador for longer than most of the other maids. She was very attractive and was always saying that life was for having fun. She had lots of fun . . . If he knew what she meant? The management didn't like staff to become friendly with guests, but some of the maids did. She didn't because she was happily married. It was odd how Lucía so often became friendly with men older than herself. Victoria claimed it was because the older men had more money. It was the kind of thing Victoria would say because she was as sour as stale vinegar. About a year ago, Lucía had met Emilio and soon he'd asked her to marry him. She'd told him she wasn't quite ready to marry, but continued going out with him. At the same time, as always, she was friendly with a succession of hotel guests who took her to expensive restaurants, the casino, and once even to

Madrid for two days. And Emilio, who was a nice man but far from bright, believed everything she told him. That was until . . .

When Edward Gates had first entered his room at the hotel, she was still in the bathroom, trying to clean the bath which was extremely dirty – management shouldn't have let the room immediately after the previous guests had left because it had been in such a state, but they never lost the chance of making an extra peseta. According to Lucía, he immediately started chatting her up and in no time suggested dinner together at whatever restaurant she cared to name. She had promised to go out with Emilio, but that didn't matter – when the Englishman returned to the hotel in the evening from wherever he'd been, she and the Englishman went to the newly opened restaurant near Deya which had recently been called the smartest on the island.

The next day at work, she had been unable to stop talking about the meal. It had cost so much, she'd been afraid he'd be furious, but it didn't seem to worry him. He was obviously very rich and so enamoured of her that she was going to enjoy a life of luxury. Things hadn't worked out as she'd hoped. He'd not taken her out again that night, which had made her furious because it looked as if far from being overwhelmingly attracted to her, he merely saw her as a convenient one-night stand. When Emilio had turned up to bother her, she must have said something which had finally made him suspicious because on the Friday morning, she had had to tell everyone she'd walked into a door. Naturally, no one had believed her.

When told Gates had skipped without paying his bill, she'd called him more names than a nice person knew and cursed him for a lying swine – which was ironic, remembering how she'd been treating Emilio. And even now she couldn't stop saying what she thought of the Englishman. Victoria said that was because she'd fallen for him and not just his money, even though he was quite a bit older, a long way from being handsome, and not all that active because of his limp . . .

'What's that?' Alvarez said sharply.

'He limped,' she said uneasily.

'Can you remember which was his bad leg?'

She shook her head.

Was this certainty, or just coincidence? (If Gates was the dead man, why had his room been cleared of all his possessions?) 'When d'you reckon a guest would choose to slip out unnoticed with all his luggage?'

'At night, when there's not many staff around.'

'So that's probably the time when someone would choose to get into the hotel?'

'I don't understand.'

'It doesn't matter . . . Will you help me?'

She hesitated.

'When you next are at the hotel, talk to the other staff and find out if anyone other than Gates was seen to go into his bedroom on Friday night or early Saturday morning.'

He stood, thanked her for her help, and left. On the drive back to Llueso, he sang an ancient song laced with Moorish influence. He had a terrible voice, but he was convinced he had identified the dead man, thanks to intelligent initiative, perseverence, and the fact he had talked to Natalia as a sop to his conscience.

Eleven

'It is a very dubious identification,' Fuster said, as he sat behind the desk. 'Many men suffer limps.'

'But not men who disappear before a body's found which has been dead for approximately the right time and which has suffered past injury that would have resulted in a limp,' Alvarez replied.

'If Gates is the dead man, why, when one presumed he was not intending to skip without paying the hotel bill, were all his personal belongings missing from the hotel bedroom?'

'The murderer knew that if they remained there, it would become logically certain that something untoward had happened to Gates and the police would be informed. By taking everything away, it made it appear that Gates was just a flyer and – as in fact happened – the odds were the hotel would not bother to make a report because of the hassle that would cause.'

'The hotel staff will have to be questioned to find out if any of them saw someone they couldn't identify who might have removed his possessions.'

'I've already arranged that. I'm also going to get from the hotel the details of his passport which can be sent to England with a request for available information.'

'You haven't already done so?'

'When I was there, I didn't know Gates limped so there

was no reason to doubt the assistant manager's assumption that he was merely a runner and very much alive.'

'Very well.'

That had been said bad-temperedly. Fuster was annoyed at being unable to deny his success, Alvarez thought as he left the room. It was cause for satisfaction. He continued along the corridor to the dark, stuffy room he was now occupying and sat. He lit a cigarette and, his thoughts romancing the possibility that Fuster was very, very annoyed, reached down to the right-hand drawer of the desk, only to discover there were no drawers. His pleasure had been so great that he'd completely forgotten he'd been forced to move from his room. What had happened to the bottle of brandy in the bottom drawer of the desk behind which Fuster now sat? With a character like his, it was even possible he'd emptied the contents down the sink . . .

After a while, Alvarez managed to reconcile himself to his loss and return to work. He used the telephone directory to find the Hotel Platjador's number, dialled that. He spoke to a secretary who, having checked with someone it was all right, gave him the information he sought.

He phoned Palma. Salas's secretary, at her most arrogant, told him to wait.

'What is it?' Salas finally demanded.

'Pursuing the investigation of the case of the unknown man found murdered, I have been making inquiries . . .'

'Did I not say that all future reports were to be made by Inspector Fuster?'

'Indeed, señor, but I judged this matter sufficiently important exceptionally to ignore your instructions.'

'If that's the case, perhaps you'll give me facts, not waffle.'

'While talking to staff at the Hotel Platjador, I learned that an Englishman, Gates, had disappeared—'

'I am far too busy to listen to what I already know.'

'But you can't—'

'Inspector Fuster, fully alive to the importance of prompt reporting, has already informed me of what you learned from inquiries made at his suggestion.'

'His suggestion? He never suggested anything. I decided the best chance of making a breakthough in identifying the dead man was to—'

'It says much that you should constantly attempt to belittle Inspector Fuster's handling of this case. Not only does it illustrate the socialistic jealousy aroused by an intelligent man doing his job excellently, it also shows that there are those who are quite unable to understand that the Cuerpo should be a team, not a number of individuals whose only concern is to promote, falsely if necessary, themselves.'

'Explain what a team is to Fuster and maybe he'll stop trying to kick his own side in the cojones.'

'A typical comment in the worst possible taste! There are occasions, and these are becoming more frequent, when I wonder if I'm right in trying to make allowances for the fact that you are a Mallorquin who was drafted into the Cuerpo before standards became sufficiently rigorous. Rest assured I shall have a close interest in this case and any further attempt on your part to denigrate Inspector Fuster, an officer whose unfailing and efficient attention to detail deserves the highest commendation, will be severely dealt with. Is that clear?'

Alvarez did not answer. Silence could be frustrating, but necessary.

'Inspector Fuster made the point that since Gates was staying at the hotel, management there will have details of his passport. These can be sent to England and the authorities asked to confirm that he is missing; if so, that we are given any available details about him that might assist us in this case. When I wondered why such details were not to hand already, Inspector Fuster very reluctantly added that when at the Hotel Platjador, you had seen no necessity to ask the management for them.'

Frustration had its limits. 'That's a load of bullshit!'

'Were you able to give the details of the Englishman's passport to Inspector Fuster when you reported to him?'

'No, but that wasn't because I forgot to ask—'

'One can only forget what one appreciates there is a need to remember.'

'It wasn't until I spoke to one of the maids—'

'I am uninterested in excuses.'

'It's fact, not excuse.'

'Surely, you allow no difference? Have you yet gained a description of Gates from the staff at the hotel and passed this on to the Institute of Forensic Pathology so that they can compare it with the physical details of the dead man?'

'No.'

'Why not?'

'Because there hasn't yet been time to suggest to Inspector Fuster that it would be a good idea to do so and give him the chance to claim the idea as his.'

The line went dead.

Dolores stepped through the bead curtain from the kitchen. 'Cousin Luisa says we are to go to lunch tomorrow.'

Alvarez cleared his throat. 'I'm still not certain what's happening—'

'I am.'

'But I may be called on to work all that day.'

'You've never found any difficulty in not working when you don't want to.'

'I've never before had Fuster doing his best to drop me into the pozo negro.'

'Why take any notice of him? He is merely an inspector; not a superior chief, not even a comisario.'

'Salas thinks there's a halo nailed to his head.'

'Cousin Luisa will be deeply hurt if you should be so misguided as not to turn up.'

'But can't you understand—?'

'It would be unbelievably rude to refuse her invitation when it is made to thank us for what some of us did.'

'Quite right,' Jaime said.

She laughed sarcastically. 'She owes you no more thanks than she owes the politicians for the food she grows and eats.'

'There's no call to go on talking like that.'

'When you drink until your words become ever more empty, I have the call to say whatever I wish.' She swept back into the kitchen.

Jaime drained his glass. 'If I could get my hands on that bloody stupid television doctor . . .'

'Just what would you do?' she demanded from the kitchen.

'I'd . . . I'd ask him what exactly he means by moderate drinking?'

'Far less than you swill.'

He looked at his empty glass and then at the bead curtain.

'Enrique, you will go to Cousin Luisa's,' she called out.

'But as I said—' Alvarez began.

'She will be cooking a special lechona.'

Lechona could make for a pleasurable meal or one so perfect that even years later it would be recalled with bated memory. If the piglet were slaughtered when the moon was in the right quarter, if each half-carcass were liberally coated with brandy, garlic, herbs, and more brandy, cooked in a wood-fired Roman oven . . . 'How good a cook is Luisa?' he asked Jaime in a low voice.

'How would I know?' Jaime replied, still resenting his wife's words.

She'd looked the kind of woman who would be an excellent cook, Alvarez decided. And surely there would be no lack of brandy to pour over the meat? Added to which, there was that malt whisky, with its indefinable, exhilarating, secret taste . . . 'I'll work out some way of making certain I'm free tomorrow,' he called out.

A clatter of dishes was her sardonic answer.

Natalia telephoned soon after he'd settled behind the drawerless desk in what was now his office. She'd spoken to almost everyone in the hotel and they couldn't be certain because there was always so much going on, but no one could recall seeing a stranger enter Gates's room.

'When you say everyone, does that include day as well as night staff?'

'Yes. I mean, those I've spoken to.'

He wasn't certain what to make of that answer. 'I forgot to ask you something. Could I get into the hotel at night without going through the reception area?'

'Not really.'

Staff were staff, no matter what the job. 'But could I?'

'Well . . .'

'Remember. Like a priest, what you tell me stops with me.'

There were two rear entrances to the hotel; one was always locked at night, the other was an emergency fire exit, supposedly only capable of being opened from the inside, but if one knew the knack . . . There was a small bar along the road which during the season never shut much before five in the morning. One or two night staff might

wander along there after the hotel bars were closed and not
have any difficulty in returning inside . . .

He thanked her, promised management would never learn
anything from him. He settled back in the chair. Someone,
knowing how to circumvent a one-way door, had entered the
hotel from the rear, gone up to Gates's room and removed all
his possessions in order to make it seem he had run without
paying his bill.

Why had Gates been murdered? Motive was usually the
key which unlocked the truth and until they knew what had
been the motive in this case, it was going to be difficult to
make any real progress. Did the extreme need to prevent
identification tell them something?

The room was very hot and stuffy and the fan was
inefficient. His eyelids drooped . . .

The telephone jerked him fully awake.

'Forensic here. We've studied the description you sent
us.'

He tried to recall what description that was.

'Obviously, there's no way we can offer a positive identification on this evidence, but if I put things another way,
it may help. I'll be very surprised if he's not your man.'

It was only after he'd replaced the receiver that his mind
cleared sufficiently to be certain what Forensic had been
talking about.

Twelve

Alvarez walked into 'his' room – as he called it in his mind – and greeted Fuster with a pleasant good morning. Fuster merely nodded a reply.

'I've some routine work that shouldn't be left until Monday,' Alvarez said.

'Why should it be?'

'Today is Saturday.'

'Which is of no account when there's work to be done.'

The man was mental, but it was not the moment to point that out since he wanted to lunch at Cousin Luisa's without having to worry. 'Naturally, work takes precedence over pleasure . . . But the point is, a case of sheep rustling has come in. I don't know how long it'll take to investigate that so I may have to break off from the murder investigation for a while . . .'

'I imagine I'll be able to survive your absence.'

'In fact, there's not much more we can do until we hear from England, is there?'

'I would say that there is much we can do. For instance, I intend to question Perello.'

'Who?' Alvarez asked, his mind on other matters.

'He was sufficiently jealous of the woman's relationship with Gates to assault her. You do not remember my telling you that?'

'I told you.'

110

'Clearly, he is a man of considerable temper and a very jealous nature. At this stage, he has to be regarded as a suspect.'

'I wouldn't agree.'

'Interesting, but of little account.'

'If Perello murdered Gates, why did he go to such lengths to prevent identification of the body?'

'I should have thought that was obvious. The moment the victim was identified, he must become the prime suspect.'

'Like Felipe Marti?'

Fuster ignored the jibe.

'Judging by what I've been told, mentally Perello's incapable of such forethought.'

'I don't follow that observation.'

'If he could plan, would he ever have allowed his jealousy to become so obvious?'

'People of small intellect have little control over their emotions.'

Alvarez mentally shrugged his shoulders. He hesitated, then said: 'Do you mind if I suggest something?'

'What?'

'That you take the questioning lightly.'

'I will conduct it in the style that has served me so well over the years.'

'The thing is, he's a Mallorquin . . .'

'I shall naturally make allowances for that.'

'And not normal mentally. If you attack him too openly, you'll confuse him to the point where he becomes virtually incoherent; if you threaten, he may well become too scared to say anything. And he—'

'There's no point in continuing.'

That was probably correct. 'Then I'll get on with my local work.' He crossed to the door.

'You didn't say where the rustling has taken place.'

He slowly turned round. Was there a cunning reason for the question? Could Fuster, by some mental alchemy, have guessed the true reason for the coming trip? If so, he needed to cover himself. 'It's difficult to be certain because the report was very vague, but I think not far from Exchau Valley.'

'An area I think you know!' Fuster chuckled. 'As we're now colleagues, working together, I'll make your task easier. If you need to cross into my territory, don't bother to get on to me for permission.'

'I'll remember that, since it may be useful. Sheep aren't sophisticated enough to worry about boundaries, so poachers don't either. There's the saying, a sheep in your flock may be worth a lamb in mine.'

'Presumably, it hasn't occurred to the peasant farmers to fence their land?'

'That's not practicable in the mountains.'

'Then why not keep sheep where they can be fenced?'

'They, along with goats, forage land which otherwise is useless.'

'If they spend their time on the mountains, it explains why the local lamb's so tough.'

The local lamb was as tender as a new bride's goodbye. Perhaps Fuster's wife was a very poor cook. It was to be hoped so.

'Very well,' Fuster said, in dismissive tones.

Alvarez left. In the room he was now occupying, he sat, yawned, looked at his watch – not quite yet time to carry out preliminary inquiries into sheep rustling in the Club Llueso. He made himself as comfortable as possible. While he had just credited Fuster with the possibility of knowing that sheep rustling was camouflage, more logical thought said this was ridiculous; but, it went on to add, authority might eventually learn he had been at Ca'n Portens. Were the visit

112

a short one, he could have been asking Miguel if any of his sheep had been lost to rustling, but if Luisa was the cook he hoped she was, the meal would be a long one and he needed a more substantial reason to explain his prolonged presence in the area when he should have been back in Llueso, working to Fuster's orders even if it was Saturday afternoon. Why not another quick visit to the Perrys before lunch? If necessary, such a visit could be represented to authority as having taken far longer than it had – and they would be the first to admit that they differed greatly when it came to judging time.

Matilde opened the front door. He introduced himself and asked if the Perrys were at home?

'They're out, but they're coming back to lunch – on Saturdays, I do the lunch unless they're away sailing.' She spoke easily, without any hint of nervousness or reserve. Plump, as so many local middle-aged women became, she had the air of someone who accepted without rancour that life distributed good and bad luck without regard to the worthiness of the recipient.

'Then I can have a word with you now.'

'Why?'

'To sort out one or two things about the Englishman who called when you were here, but the Perrys weren't.'

'I suppose you'd best come in, then.'

She led the way into the sitting-room and they sat. He said: 'Was this Englishman here just over three weeks ago – or was it considerably longer?'

She thought for a while, her gaze unfocussed; although her face was now lined and her skin blemished, it was possible to discern that when young, she had been attractive. 'More like three weeks.'

'What can you tell me about the Englishman?'

'Not enough to fill a thimble. I mean, he only spoke

English and although I know a bit through working for
foreigners – not that the señor agrees! – it's difficult. Still,
he understood Señor Perry wasn't here.'

'He asked for the señor by name?'

'That's right.'

'What did he say when you told him the señor was
away?'

'Asked when he'd be back. I said, they was off on
their yacht to somewhere and I couldn't say when they'd
return.'

'Did the Englishman suggest he'd call again some other
time?'

'Not as I remember.'

'What happened next?'

'He left,' she answered, surprised he should ask so
obvious a question.

'Describe him.'

'I'm no good at that sort of thing,' she protested.

'I know it's very difficult, but do the best you can.'

'He was maybe the same age as the señor – though the
señor isn't as old as he says, judging by the way he looked
at a señorita who was here the other day.'

'My cousin insists a man only loses interest when he's
dead . . . What sort of face did he have?'

She spoke slowly, frequently becoming briefly silent,
occasionally correcting herself, but finally presenting him
with a word picture of some substance. The Englishman
was quite tall and slightly built; his round face was topped
with black hair that wasn't exactly curly, but certainly was
wavy; he'd very blue eyes, a bit of a nose, and nice even,
white teeth; many women would call him handsome, but
she wouldn't; his type thought too much of themselves and
so couldn't be trusted – not where women were concerned,
that was. There was that look about him . . .

114

A description that in a few essentials was similar to the one he'd gained from the staff at the Hotel Platjador.

'Oh! There is one more thing,' she added. 'He limped.'

Eureka! An unknown Englishman no longer. Gates. He had certainly called at the house on the Thursday and possibly on the Wednesday evening when there was no one there; and on the Friday?

His feeling of success faded. His original inquiries at this house had been made to try to identify the Englishman who would provide Miguel with an alibi of sorts to satisfy the sargento. That identification had just been completed, but in doing this all chance of helping Miguel was lost. Would Dolores understand? Would she allow herself to understand?

'Have I said something wrong?' Matilde asked uncertainly.

'Nothing. I was just thinking.'

There were sounds from the hall and a moment later, Iris entered. She came to so abrupt a stop that her husband banged into her.

'Sorry, darling,' he said, as he stepped back. 'I wasn't expecting you to put on the brakes. Have I hurt you?'

She shook her head.

He moved round her. 'They say disorganized families are becoming more common.'

'I hope the señora is all right?' Alvarez said.

'Yes,' she answered briefly.

Matilde hurriedly stood. 'He wanted to ask me questions,' she said in flustered Spanish.

'How's that?' Perry questioned in English.

Alvarez said in English. 'She is worried you may be annoyed that when you returned, we were sitting in here. But I needed to ask her one or two things and it seemed more sensible to sit in comfort than to stand.'

'Of course. For goodness sake, tell her not worry.'

'What questions?' Iris demanded.

Her husband said jovially: 'Never mind the non-essentials, let's concentrate on what really matters. Inspector, what will you drink?'

He hesitated. He might soon be enjoying more of that extraordinary, unforgettable malt whisky. If so, there would for once be point to remembering that strange dictum – present abstinence enhances future pleasure. But Miguel had been so furious that Luisa had produced the whisky, he might today offer only a very ordinary brandy in order to give the impression of honest poverty . . .

'I can't tempt you?'

How did one resist temptation? 'Perhaps just a small coñac with ice would be very pleasant.'

Perry turned to his wife. 'Would you be bartender?'

She hesitated, then said: 'What do you want?'

'A G and T, please.'

She went through to the kitchen, followed by Matilde.

Perry sat. 'I haven't looked at the thermometer out on the patio, but I'm sure today's even hotter. I feel sorry for anyone who has to work in such conditions. One of the pleasures of being at sea is that even if you're on the equator, things never become this oppressive and sticky . . . I think you told my wife that you weren't a sailor? You're missing a lot!' He chatted about the joys of sailing.

Iris returned. She handed a glass to Alvarez, one to her husband, sat. Matilde came through from the kitchen and wished them goodbye.

'See you on Monday,' Perry said.

She smiled uncertainly, left.

As they heard the front door shut, Perry said. 'We talk to each other and seldom have any understanding.

116

Still, that can happen when two people speak the same language.'

'Not really,' Iris said.

'Yes, really. Remember what someone wrote. England and America are two nations divided by a common language. You can say something totally respectable in Britain which will earn you a face slap in America.' He turned to Alvarez. 'I've been told there's the same room for misunderstanding with Castilian and South American Spanish?'

'That is very true, señor. Occasionally, grave offence occurs.'

'Probably, usually by people who lack any sense of humour.'

Alvarez heard a clock strike once. Although lunch would not be served at Ca'n Portens for at least another two hours, it would be ridiculous to arrive too late to enjoy more than one drink of malt whisky – if Miguel had decided to play the part of a good host. 'Señor, I must leave very soon, but perhaps I might first ask you a question?'

'Of course. Presumably, this is something to do with the Englishman who called when we weren't here?'

'That is so.'

'Fire away.'

'Have you thought who he might have been?'

'Repeatedly, without any success.'

'And I am right when I say he never returned?'

Perry smiled. 'Had he done so, I'd be able to identify him.'

'Have you ever heard of a man called Gates?'

There was a gasp from Iris.

Perry said quickly: 'As you'll have gathered, you've touched a raw nerve. John Gates was a cousin of Iris's and they were brought up together after his widowed mother died so that he became far more brother than cousin. They

117

were a family dogged by tragedy and he died in a car crash just under a year ago. As you can see, Iris still finds a mention of him very sad.'

'Naturally, I am sorry this should have caused so much distress, but I was not referring to the señora's cousin.'

'Was that, then, also the name of the Englishman who called here several weeks ago?'

'We think so.'

'An unfortunate coincidence.'

'Indeed. And I am so sorry,' Alvarez said for the second time.

'You weren't to know,' she said. 'And although it was a bit of a shock for a moment, it doesn't upset me now as it would have done.'

'I am glad of that, señora.' Alvarez spoke to Perry once more. 'Are you sure it was considerably more than three weeks ago when Matilde told you the Englishman had called here?'

'You sound as if you have reason to think I must be wrong?'

'It seems that that is so, señor.'

'Then I'll accept the possibility, but, hanging on to male superiority as hard as I can, not the probability . . . Your glass is empty. May I refill it?'

'Thank you, but I must leave.' He stood.

'If this other Gates ever does turn up again, I'll let you know,' Perry said, as he came to his feet.

'I am afraid there is no chance of that, señor. He has been murdered.'

'Oh! . . . Then your questions were a lot sharper than they appeared to be.'

'I am merely trying to trace the movements of Gates before he was killed.'

'I see . . . Or perhaps I am meant to see. Please accept it

as a compliment, Inspector, when I say you are far sharper than first impressions might suggest.'

Which, Alvarez thought as he said goodbye, had the outline of a double-edged compliment.

Thirteen

M unar, far less surly than usual, offered them whisky and winked as he said that he'd found a bottle floating on the tideline. Having tasted the whisky, Jaime suggested they went down to whichever tideline and looked to see if any more bottles had drifted inshore.

The lechona was as good as any Alvarez had ever tasted – the crackling fractured at the first bite and the meat, suffused with the miraculous touch of herbs and brandy, seemed to melt in the mouth. As he finished his second large helping, he made the mistake of complimenting Luisa so extravagantly that Dolores became annoyed. The Marqués de Murrieta was bottled sunshine. The castello de turron was so rich that neither Juan nor Isabel could finish what was on the dish. After drinking his second Bisquit Dubouche, Alvarez lazily wondered if, despite his present job, he would be accepted in the smuggling fraternity.

One law of life decreed that the more perfect this moment, the more imperfect the next. Alvarez had not been home for more than ten minutes when there was a phone call from the Police Local in the port. They had been trying to contact him for the past two hours to say that there had been reports of four snatched handbags and clearly a small gang was at work. He suggested that, despite the number of thefts, these had probably been carried out by different individuals –

when the case would have been theirs to handle – but the speaker argued forcibly that witness evidence pointed to the fact that the same three people had carried out each theft which meant the case was his. When he replaced the receiver, he thought bitterly how there were always people who tried to palm off their work on to others.

He drove down to the port and spoke to the senior duty municipal policeman. As he began to explain, eyewitness evidence was notoriously inaccurate— He was interrupted. In each case, a badly dressed woman offered a bunch of roses for sale and when the victim, touched by the apparent need for compassion, opened her handbag to give some money, it was snatched; on each occasion, she had been in the company of a man with a scar on the cheek who was clearly one of her accomplices, ready to block any pursuit of the second man to whom the handbag had been passed immediately after the actual theft. Those, said the policeman, were the facts.

Alvarez left the station in a bad temper and made his way to the front where he strolled among the crowds, searching for a woman who offered roses and two men whose unusually sharp awareness of everything and everyone around them would identify them to him. By the time he reached the ice cream stall at the eastern arm of the harbour, he was hot, weary, and wondering how soon he could reasonably decide the thieves had moved on to, hopefully, a resort in someone else's territory. He bought a double cornet.

'So what's brought you down here?'

He turned to face Rivera, one of the assistant harbour-masters. 'I'm searching for someone.'

'I've seen people search harder.'

'Take life gently and live to be a hundred.'

'From the look of you, you're aiming for a hundred and twenty . . . You can buy me an ice cream.'

'I've no money left.'

He turned to the stallholder. 'You'll give him credit, won't you?'

'When I aim to stay in business?'

'Then I'll have to treat myself. Give me a double one like he's got, chocolate and pistachio.' When served, he joined Alvarez in the small patch of shade the stall provided. 'So how are things these days?'

'I suppose things could be worse.'

'Sounds as if you can't think how.'

'I'm having to work with another inspector.'

'What's his problem?'

'Himself.'

They became silent as they ate. Alvarez stared out at the eastern side of the bay and the beauty of the sea, mountains, and cloudless sky worked their usual magic – what signified the pinpricks when one lived with the gods?

Beyond the small promontory on which had once stood a mansion where, rumour still insisted, saturnalian nights had been enjoyed, a crimson-hulled yacht came into sight, her spinnaker only kept full with difficulty because the sea breeze, which had recently sprung up, was so slight.

'She's a real beauty,' Rivera said.

Alvarez turned to look at the sunbathers on the beach to his left.

'You've the mind of a fifteen-year-old. I'm talking about the ketch.'

He looked to his right. Inshore were two small sailing dinghies, offshore, three catamarans. 'The one with the multi-coloured sail?'

'Are you saying you think that's a ketch?'

'How would I know what it is?'

'By getting an education. Don't ever set out to sail the seven seas – you'll run aground before you've reached Cap

Parelona. I'm talking about the ketch which has just come through the heads.'

He looked out and saw the yacht which aroused Rivera's enthusiasm. Convinced landlubber that he was, he had to admit that she was a thing of great beauty. 'There's something about it looks familiar.'

'I doubt that. And a yacht is always she, not it.'

He watched her ghost along.

'In her, you can laugh at gale force nine,' Rivera said. 'There aren't many I really envy, but I do them that own yachts like her. Most especially when they're not up to handling them. Still, the couple who have her pass. If you knew anything, which you don't, you'd tell they're seamen from the way the spinnaker's full when there's so little breeze. Like as not, it's the wife at the helm; the husband can be a bit granny-knot at times. Pleasant enough otherwise. Can't speak Spanish, of course, but he doesn't start shouting when you have trouble understanding what he's after. Funny people, foreigners. Some of 'em think they can walk on water.'

'Where's the harm in that? One day they'll try and drown.' Alvarez ate the end of the cornet into which, with his tongue, he had wedged the last portion of chocolate ice cream. 'I'd better start moving.'

'Give my regards to Dolores and Jaime.'

'And mine to María.' He moved out of the shade into the full sunlight, came to a halt. 'Is that yacht called *Argo*?'

'Something like that.'

'And people called Perry own her?'

'That's right.'

'There's a picture of her on the wall of the place where the Perrys live.'

'Surprised you didn't reckon you were looking at a coaling barge.'

123

'It's the bright colour of the hull I noticed first.'

'That's what you need to highlight the boat when you've been demasted and are starting to founder and if you aren't rescued real quick, you're going to go down with her.'

'People spend money to risk that?'

'Only those with red blood in their veins.'

'And very little anything between their ears.'

Fourteen

It seemed to Alvarez that the Good Lord had been guilty of inequitable judgment when He'd decreed it was only the seventh day on which man should not work. Why not a couple of other days as well to even up things? He lay in bed, sheet thrown back, fan switched on to full speed, and stared up at the ceiling on which a pattern of sunshine, thrown up through the closed shutters by a reflective surface, shimmered. A masochist would probably argue it was by having only one in seven days off that the seventh was fully appreciated; masochists never did themselves as much harm as others would have wished . . .

Downstairs, the phone rang. He checked the time. Ten o'clock on a Sunday morning – only a woman could be so insensitive as to ring at such a time on such a day.

'Enrique,' Dolores shouted from downstairs.

'What?'

'What d'you think? The call is for you.'

He cursed the caller. He slowly swivelled round on the bed, put his feet into slippers and, since he wore only trousers – Dolores required the proprieties to be observed at all times – slipped on a cotton dressing-gown.

At the foot of the stairs, he called out. 'Who is it?'

'He didn't say,' she answered from the kitchen. 'And I didn't recognize the voice.'

He continued through to the front room, picked up the receiver. 'Yes?'

'Why aren't you here?'

He also failed to recognize the voice. 'Where's here?'

'What are you doing there?'

'Where's there?'

'I now understand what the superior chief meant when he said that there were times when talking to you was like trying to find the way out of a maze.'

Fuster! On a Sunday morning! 'If you'd said who you were, there would have been only open pastures. Is there a problem?'

'You are not here. Which, I hasten to add, is at the post.'

'It's Sunday.'

'When there is work to be done, the day is immaterial.'

Alvarez stared at the small pottery kitten which had stood on the mantelpiece in the central position of honour since Isabel had given it to Dolores on the previous Mother's Day. It seemed to be smiling.

'You are to come to the office immediately.'

'Why?'

'We have just received a report from England.'

Was it hypocrisy or a love of perversion which made the English disregard the customs of civilized countries and transmit reports on a Sunday? 'Why should that cause mayhem?'

'You have forgotten our request for information concerning Edward Gates? It is a long report and you will need to study it carefully before, on the basis of what you learn from it, continuing your part of the investigation.'

'Why can't that wait until tomorrow?'

'A ridiculous question.'

He almost made the mistake of asking why.

*　　*　　*

126

Fuster was in 'Alvarez's' room; on top of the desk was a single folder alongside which, placed with geometric precision, were three sheets of a fax message. Alvarez sat on the edge of the desk in the hopes that this introduction of untidiness would annoy.

'It's taken you long enough to get here,' Fuster observed.

'I had to have some breakfast.'

He looked at his wristwatch, raised his eyebrows, pursed his lips, then gestured at the message. 'It's been translated and is in Spanish although the grammar suggests a degree of illiteracy. Nevertheless, perhaps they are thinking of becoming Europeans.'

Alvarez reached across for the three sheets, read.

Following a conventional upbringing, Edward Terrence Gates had joined the police force and, after the statutory two years' probation, had been appointed a police constable. In succeeding years, he had twice received a chief constable's commendation for courage, had passed sergeant's exams with sufficiently high marks to be noted as a candidate for the accelerated promotion course which had recently been initiated by the county force, had been sent to Beaconhurst House.

(Would the members of the Cuerpo General de Policia please be kind enough to treat the following personal information as strictly confidential. Obviously, it would be most unfortunate if the facts became widely known.)

Superintendent Hartley, a man of deserved reputation, had been in command at Beaconhurst House. Unfortunately, a relationship had developed between his wife and Gates which had gone undetected for a while; then, due to a sudden change of plans, the superintendent had returned home unexpectedly to be faced by obvious evidence of his wife's adultery. There had been a fight in the course of which both men had suffered injuries, Gates's being the more serious – a badly broken leg. For the sake of discipline, the matter had been hushed up; Gates had been informed that he could no longer look for promotion and he had resigned the force.

He had joined Steadfast Security, a firm which dealt with industrial security and also carried out private investigations. His work was highly regarded. His personal reputation was that of a womaniser, but since there had never been any complaints from clients on this score, management had not had occasion to become concerned. At the beginning of this year, a Mr Basil Perry . . .

'Well I'll be a fairy queen!'

'What is it?' Fuster asked.

'Perry appears!'

'Why should that be significant?'

'He claims never to have met or heard of Gates.'

'How do you know that?'

'It's what he told me yesterday.'

'Who is he and why—' The phone interrupted Fuster.

Alvarez resumed reading.

Perry had requested Steadfast Security to determine the nature of his wife's relationship with Ivor Keen. They'd first met Keen at a cocktail party in Henley and a friendship had developed. Perry's wife had found him open, warm, and sophisticatedly amusing from the beginning; Perry had been less enthusiastic and soon had begun to suspect that under the guise of the lighthearted relationship, Keen was having an affair with his wife. He wanted the firm to determine whether his suspicions were justified. Asked if he had questioned her about the nature of the relationship, he replied that he had not; he might be mistaken and if so, what would she think of him for harbouring such suspicions? (Trying to sit on the fence and finding it too sharp for comfort, was the unnecessary and unprofessional comment.)

Gates had been put in charge of the investigation and from time to time he'd called on other operators to help since Perry had specified he wanted facts rather than probabilities and a modest bill. A close watch was kept on Iris Perry's lifestyle for a reasonable length of time and at the conclusion, Gates's report was to the effect that although a strong friendship clearly existed between the two, there was nothing to suggest this had a sexual basis. At no time had the two been seen to seek out circumstances where sex would be easy e.g. on one occasion, Perry had been away from home and Keen had visited Mrs Perry in the evening and they had remained, fully clothed, either in the dining- or the sitting-room until he left at a relatively early hour.

Perry had refused to accept the evidence in the report as proof of his wife's fidelity. (The senior partner had at this stage wondered if he were suffering from some form of persecution complex; nothing had subsequently occurred to give credence to the possibility.) He wanted the surveillance to continue even though it was put to him that it did seem this would be both a waste of their time and his money. He suggested that he would tell his wife he intended to make a long, solo voyage in his yacht. Knowing he could not suddenly turn up, the two would almost certainly be off their guard and become careless.

Perry had set sail. During the following period, his wife had not once met Keen. Then she had told the housekeeper that she'd spoken to her husband by phone and he wanted her to join him down in Biarritz; she'd added that they intended sailing into the Mediterranean and staying there to escape the English winter; the housekeeper's wages would be sent to her by their solicitors, who would also deal with any problems that might arise.

The senior partner, an optimistic sentimentalist despite his job, had assumed that being on his own in the immensity and solitude of the ocean, Perry had managed to regain a sense of proportion and so rid his mind of the corrupting suspicions which had haunted it; also, although he probably would never admit this, he wanted to give his wife a long holiday as an unspoken apology.

The senior partner's wholesome beliefs were dented, if not shattered, when a fax was received the day after Mrs Perry left which asked for the final report to be sent poste restante, Palma de Mallorca. This request not only disillusioned, it also raised a problem when, thinking the case was at an end, a request for the settlement of the account, less the amount originally received as a deposit, was made to the solicitors. Without specific authority, they'd replied, they could (or was it would?) not settle the account. The bill could have been sent with the report, but the use of a post restante address meant that it might be some considerable time before it was seen and, rich men being poor payers unless it was in their interests to be good ones, there might very well be a long wait before settlement; in the meantime the bank was, as always, charging a high rate of interest.

Gates had suggested a possible solution. He'd booked a month's stay (he was owed holiday time from the previous year) in Mallorca. Why shouldn't he combine a little business with a lot of pleasure and try to find if Perry was on the island – his yacht would provide a ready means of tracing him. And what could be more tactful than to say he had sought Perry out on behalf of the company to present the report because they were sure he would wish to have the good news it contained (i.e. that his wife had not seen Keen once during his absence so that the previous assessment of the relationship was confirmed in spades) at the first possible opportunity and only then, very discreetly, add that there was the firm's bill to settle and an immediate cheque would be very welcome.

Gates had gone on holiday and nothing more had been heard from him. At the office, they'd thought he'd been unable to find Perry, Perry had stalled paying, or all had gone as planned and so he saw no need to advise them of that fact. Whichever, no one had been concerned when he'd failed to turn up on the day he was due back at work since returning staff often complained of having been delayed by grounded planes, shipwrecks, tornadoes, or floods. However, as the days slipped by . . . Then they'd learned that he had been murdered . . .

When he'd finished reading the report, Fuster was still talking over the phone on what was, evidently, a personal call. Alvarez would have liked to remind the other that personal calls to the office were officially forbidden, but such a reminder might well turn into a boomerang in the future. He slid off the desk, put down the fax, and began to walk towards the door.

Fuster put his hand over the mouthpiece. 'Hang on.'

He crossed to the chair which had replaced the one with a broken leg and sat. It was about the time, he thought gloomily, when one normally had the first Sunday morning drink.

Fuster finally replaced the receiver. 'You say Perry denies knowing Gates?'

'I said, Perry claims not to know who Gates was.'

'How can you be certain of that?'

'He said so.'

'Why?'

'You have more questions than a dog has fleas.'

'But so far, no answers. Have you been carrying on an investigation which involves Perry?'

'No.'

'Then why should you have spoken to him, why should he have told you he did not know Gates?'

'It was with reference to something else.'

'What?'

'It was not an official investigation.'

'You wish to call it an unofficial investigation?'

'A friendly discussion.'

'Yesterday, you told me that you needed to investigate a report of sheep rustling. Does Perry keep sheep?'

'I rather doubt it.'

'Then why did you question him yesterday?'

'I didn't say I did.'

'Did you?'

'I spoke to him.'

'Why? How could an Englishman who owns no sheep assist you in identifying sheep rustlers who were obviously Mallorquins?'

'Englishmen rustle sheep.'

'In England.'

'They've exported several of their other objectionable habits.'

'I reckon your questioning of Señor Perry had nothing to do with sheep.'

'A man can reckon anything he likes provided he's ready to face the reckoning.'

'The superior chief told me he was very concerned because it seemed you had been helping a relation who was almost certainly guilty of smuggling. I think your meeting with Señor Perry was somehow connected with that.'

'Are you hoping for a half-price case of malt whisky?'

'Is that what was being smuggled?'

Alvarez silently swore – how could he have become so

annoyed by the other's pomposity that he had inadvertently mentioned the whisky? 'How would I know what it was?'

'It is greatly to be hoped for the sake of the Cuerpo that you don't.'

'If I were in that racket, I'd live in a manor house and drive a Range Rover.'

'Not if you were smart enough to hide your ill-gotten gains – as I understand Munar is.'

'Surely the superior chief has repeatedly told you I couldn't begin to be that smart?'

'Unless you use your apparent stupidity as a cloak.'

His apparent stupidity . . . About to reply angrily to the insult, he accepted that to do so would be a mistake. 'You're climbing the wrong mountain. Miguel had an alibi which proved he couldn't have been handling the smuggled goods, but he couldn't corroborate this. All I've been trying to do is uncover that corroboration. It's our duty to protect innocence as rigorously as we pursue guilt.'

'When, one needs to add, innocence lies in the eyes of the law as well as those of the beholder.'

'Gates would have provided that corroboration.'

'Then it is unfortunate for Munar that he died. Or would it perhaps be more accurate to say, fortunate?'

'What are you suggesting?'

'Munar claims Gates could have supported his alibi. Why should he not be lying? He discovered Gates was honest and wouldn't support his lie. Since this left him wide open to being convicted of smuggling, he decided Gates had to die.'

'Which would mean he was no better off; in fact, a damn sight worse because if convicted, he'll spend far more time inside than if just taken for smuggling, which is a very minor offence.'

'Only a Mallorquin would claim that.'

133

'Because we have suffered so much over the centuries, we have learned a sense of proportion.' Alvarez brought a pack of cigarettes from his pocket.

'I'd rather you did not smoke in here.'

He struck a match and lit a cigarette.

'You hardly help yourself with your attitude.'

'On the contrary, it makes me feel much happier.'

Fuster's voice rose in tone, but he still spoke calmly. 'Why did Perry deny he knew who Gates was?'

'I've no idea.'

'You didn't think it reasonable to find out?'

'When I spoke to him, there was no reason to believe he was lying.'

'There is now.'

'As I've just pointed out.'

'Question him this afternoon and find out why he lied.'

On Sunday afternoon? 'He's a rich foreigner which means he believes afternoons were invented for sleeping off liquid lunches. Interrupt his dreams and accuse him of lying and—'

'Have you never discovered the art of subtlety?'

'Be as twistedly subtle as a politician seeking re-election and it'll still very soon become obvious he's not being offered an address of welcome.'

'Clearly, it would be far better if I handled the matter, but unfortunately that is not possible. This afternoon, I intend to question Perello again.'

'Again? I'd no idea you'd actually done so already.'

'There was no reason to inform you of the fact. I am questioning him at length because he can offer no alibi, he has a strong motive for murder, is known to be violent, and continually contradicts himself.'

'Don't place any emphasis on the contradictions since he's virtually simple.'

'Or sufficiently intelligent to understand the value of apparent simplicity.'

What a pleasure it would be, Alvarez thought, to watch Fuster choke on his own smug superiority.

Fifteen

Alvarez awoke and wondered why he was so certain the world had turned grey. Then he remembered that instead of enjoying the rest of the day, he had been told to drive to Ca'n Isault to question Perry. There was further annoyance in the knowledge that it was largely his own fault that this was so. If he'd had the sense to keep quiet when he'd read the name 'Perry' in the report from England; hadn't been so struck by the fact Perry had denied knowing who Gates was; had allowed himself a little thought . . . The report from England had specifically mentioned direct contact only between Perry and the senior partner, which was logical – a client dealt with the boss, the boss gave the orders to the operatives. If Gates had kept a discreet surveillance – which one must presume he had – then there was every possibility Perry had never knowingly seen him, far less spoken to him. So Perry's denial might very well be the truth. And yet . . . Iris had been shocked to hear the name 'Gates'. Perry had covered her reaction by suggesting her cousin of the same name had recently died. Quite a coincidence! And there were other incidents which could be viewed from different angles. Judging time could be difficult. Perry, seemingly an easy-going person who wouldn't normally be worried by much, had been at considerable pains to persuade his wife that her estimate of how long it had been since the Englishman had called at their house was wrong; yet her estimate had been supported by Matilde. Could his insistence mean he'd been trying to establish the Englishman could not have been Gates? On the first visit he had made to Ca'n Isault, Iris had opened the front door and greeted him normally until he identified himself as a detective – she had been shocked. At the time, he'd judged this was because of the strange English respect for the law and consequent fear of breaking it even in the most minor matters. Had her fear had a far more concrete basis? On a subsequent visit, she'd been startled to see him in the sitting-room, talking to Matilde; she had 'frozen' and her husband had crashed into her. Just surprise, even if somewhat exaggerated, or something more?

These were questions which certainly needed answering and Fuster had told him to find out what those answers were . . . Now. But Fuster was no yachtsman and therefore it would not have occurred to him that a Sunday was the perfect day to take to the water. The odds surely had to be that the *Argo* was somewhere out at sea and therefore a trip to Ca'n Isault would prove a wasted journey. What was more polluting than that? . . . He closed his eyes. The afternoon ceased to be grey.

On Monday morning, Alvarez had just settled behind the desk in what was now his room when Fuster rushed in. 'You're finally here, then.'

'I am, therefore I think.'

'You keep unconventional hours.'

'Only in the sense that they are far longer than most endure.'

'When I arrived, you were not here; nor were you, half an hour later.'

'I left home expecting to arrive here several minutes before the official time – I always find it advantageous to have a brief moment of quiet reflection before actually starting work. However, I was waylaid by a man who often gives me useful information and I decided that it would be to the point to find out if he could tell me anything of consequence, so I spent some considerable while with him.'

'In the Club Llueso?'

'I normally never go there during working hours.'

'I've heard otherwise.'

'Rumours are lies clothed with a perverse chuckle.'

'Have you entered the information gained from this man in your crime diary?'

'I learned nothing useful. Shall I write a nought?'

'I dislike facetiousness.'

'How else does one survive the job?'

'By working much harder.'

'Some cures are worse than the diseases.'

'How do you imagine the superior chief would greet such a negative attitude?'

'No doubt I'll find out as soon as you have passed on the information.'

'It is hardly surprising that he recently said to me—' He stopped.

'Said what?'

'It was spoken in confidence.'

'Of your enjoyment at hearing it?'

'Did you question Señor Perry yesterday afternoon?' Fuster snapped.

'When I rang the front door bell at Ca'n Isault, there was no response. Either they were sleeping so soundly – fortunate people! – that they didn't hear the chimes or, more likely, they were on their yacht. I thought I'd return this morning.'

'It has been "this morning" for a long time already.' Fuster

138

began to fidget with his right sideburn. 'I'm not convinced there is point to your returning to question him. There is very little room for doubting that Perello killed Gates.'

'How's that?'

'When a man can't look you in the face, becomes more and more nervous, repeatedly contradicts himself, and talks ever wilder nonsense, one can be reasonably confident one is dealing with guilt.'

'Unless the victim is far more simple than one is willing to allow.'

'As I have previously suggested, simple-mindedness is often used as camouflage.'

'Natalia at the Platjador reckons it's not camouflage.'

'You accept the opinion of a hotel maid?'

'Often more willingly than that of a professional psychiatrist since her judgment comes free of charge. Would it help if I had a word with Perello?'

'I very much doubt it.'

'He is more likely to open up to me, as a fellow Mallorquin.'

'You can confine yourself to questioning Señor Perry.'

'You said, a moment ago, that wasn't necessary.'

'I said I was not certain it was necessary. When there is uncertainty, a good detective checks until certainty is established.' He crossed to the door, then turned back. 'You can also take the opportunity to question Munar; officially this time.'

'Smuggling is the Guardia's pigeon.'

'You will question him to determine whether he should be regarded as a possible suspect.'

'Your certainty regarding Perello seems to be becoming less certain every minute.'

'I can hardly expect you to understand that whilst one

may be convinced of guilt, until one can prove that, one has to consider all other possibilities.' Fuster left.

Alvarez slumped back in the chair. If, as Fuster maintained, cleverness could be concealed by assumed stupidity, how far could stupidity be concealed by assumed cleverness?

Luisa was in the vegetable garden, using a hose connected to a distant estanque, kept filled from a nearby well, to water a ragged row of French beans. As Alvarez left the car, the dog appeared and barked, then slunk away as she shouted. He approached her. The labour involved in growing anything on such poor, exhausted soil would never be justified by results, but he understood that it was the peasant background which drove her; a peasant, so the old saw suggested, would try to grow cayenne peppers in hell. He complimented her on the beans. She knew the words were false, but was still grateful for them.

'Is Miguel around?'

She shook her head, moved the hose.

'Will he be returning soon?'

'Maybe; maybe not.'

Years ago, to know anything for certain was to place oneself at risk. He looked beyond the house at the face of the mountain. Somewhere on the stark, often precipitous slopes there was almost certainly a cave, with well-concealed entrance, in which were many cases of twenty-year-old malt whisky, many cases of Bisquit Dubouche cognac, many cases of American cigarettes, and only a few knew what else.

'Why do you want him?' she asked.

'To have a chat about the Englishman who called here that Wednesday evening. You've heard what happened to him?'

She shook her head.

'He was murdered and had his head and hands cut off to try to prevent identification.'

She seemed unmoved; she had learned to accept with bowed shoulders the worst that life could offer. 'You'll want something to drink.' It was a statement, not a question. 'I'll turn the water off.'

'I'll do that.' He skirted the beans, passed between rows of sweet peppers, some green, some turning red, all small, and then walked parallel to vines which were doing well and had many large bunches of grapes that were swelling. Vines were successful on poor soil. He reached the estanque and turned off the stopcock. He met Luisa at the front door of the house and followed her up the stairs to the main room. She asked him what he'd like to drink. He sat. There was a scrabbling sound and the dog appeared at the head of the stairs, then came forward, belly close to the ground, tail almost out straight, ready to run or turn nasty. When a metre from where he sat, it hesitated, mouth open, large teeth showing proudly as it panted. He held out his right hand and it very slowly moved forward again until he could fondle its ears. It settled on its haunches, tail waving across the floor.

She returned with two glasses, one fuller than the other. 'It's not everyone he'll talk to,' she said, as she handed him a glass. 'The sargento is real scared of him,' she added with simple pleasure.

He drank. If he ever won the lottery, or took to smuggling, he'd enjoy malt whisky of this quality at every available opportunity. 'Luisa, you have to realize that since the Englishman is dead, he can't say he was here, talking to Miguel, while the smuggling was going on.'

'Does that matter?'

'He would have corroborated Miguel's evidence and the sargento would have had to believe that.'

'Miguel was here; I told the sargento.'

'A wife's word isn't sufficient because if she's a good wife, she'll always lie to save her husband.'

She thought for a while. 'Maybe they will take him away to prison?'

'That all depends on the evidence they have that implicates him. As far as I know, there's just the word of one informer and that won't be enough. But perhaps someone else will also say Miguel was on the beach, helping to unload.'

'He was here.'

'But there isn't the proof he was.'

'They'll put him in jail?' she asked a second time.

When he saw the fear in her eyes, he wished he could deny the possibility, but the truth had to be spoken. 'It could happen. The sargento must be a determined man.'

'They'll cage him, like he was an animal?'

He didn't answer.

'You must tell the sargento to stop,' she said, her voice rising.

'If I tried to do that, I'd cause more harm than good.'

'Miguel would die in prison.' She drank so quickly, liquid spilled down her chin.

He accepted the possibility that she was right. When a man had lived the freedom of the mountains, imprisonment could easily be a death sentence.

'Angel will say,' she cried out.

'Angel?'

'He will tell that Miguel was here.'

'I don't understand.'

'He was here, when the Englishman drove up.'

'Then why the hell didn't Miguel say so at the beginning?' Alvarez asked, his voice expressing his bewilderment. 'Then there would have been no need to search for the Englishman.'

'He . . . We wasn't to say, whatever happened. But Miguel can't go to jail.'

'What is Angel's surname? I must talk to him to make certain he will corroborate Miguel's evidence.'

'Angel Gomilio Balle . . . Tell him Miguel musn't go to jail.'

'I'll do what I can. Where does he live?'

'Sa Setri.'

Sixteen

As he entered Almerich Valley, Alvarez couldn't stop hoping he was adding two and two together and making five. Perhaps Angel Gomilio – these days, the second surname was being dropped – was just an ordinary farmer. But if so, wouldn't Miguel have named him from the beginning? Logic said Gomilio was a known member of the smuggling gang and the knowledge of his presence at Ca'n Portens would have made Miguel's protestations of innocence as trustworthy as a shepherd's claim that the lamb bearing his neighbour's brand had wandered into the flock during the night. The odds against the Englishman's telling anyone in authority that Gomilio had been at the farm must have seemed very remote, but professional criminals (for the moment, allowing that smuggling was a criminal action) remained at large only if they constantly allowed that the impossible might happen and the unlikely would. Gomilio might well be a man who saw murder as the simplest form of insurance. Would Miguel have been all that reluctant to have a part in the killing of a man who might threaten his freedom?

He braked to a halt outside Ca'n Isault. Perhaps he would persuade Perry to admit he had recognized Gates, thereby arming with significance those incidents which otherwise had none. How readily, he realized, one would wish ill on a relative stranger if to do so would be to release a friend . . .

Perry opened the front door. 'Nice to see you,' he said, sounding as if he meant his words.

'I'm sorry to trouble you yet again . . .'

'No trouble. Come on in.'

He entered.

'Iris,' Perry called out.

'I'm here,' she replied from a distant room.

'Inspector Alvarez has arrived.'

A friendly acknowledgment or a warning?

'Let's go through to the sitting-room,' Perry said. 'You should find it cooler than the last time you were here because we've bought a mobile air-conditioner even though we may not be around long enough to make all that much use of it.'

'You are thinking of leaving?'

'Iris wants to stay, I'm becoming very restless. The Greek islands are singing their sirens' song . . . Probably because I've never seen them. Romantic illusions make for the itchiest feet. Do sit. And tell me what you'd like to drink?'

'May I have a coñac and ice?'

'A man of infinite custom,' Perry said, smiling.

Only when there wasn't twenty-year-old malt whisky on offer.

As Perry left by one doorway, Iris entered through the other. 'Hullo,' she said brightly.

Alvarez stood. 'Good morning, señora.'

'Do sit. Is Basil getting you a drink?'

'He is, thank you.'

She called out: 'Basil, will you pour me a glass of champagne, please?'

'To hear is to obey.'

'I'll remember that!'

Was the cheerful atmosphere natural or forced? He

couldn't decide. 'Have you been sailing recently?' he asked.

'We were out all yesterday.'

Obviously, forethought had saved him a wasted journey the previous day. There was a measure of self-congratulation to be gained from that.

'There was so little wind that to say we were sailing is an exaggeration, but who can reasonably complain when there isn't a cloud in the sky? Beyond the heads, the water is still crystal clear and when I went snorkling, I saw an enormous fish – I'm sure it was as long as I'm tall.'

'Undoubtedly, a great white shark,' Perry said, as he returned, a tray in his hands. He handed her a flute.

'Why won't you believe me when I say how big it was?'

'Because in my youth, I did a lot of fishing.' He handed Alvarez a glass. 'Are you a keen fisherman?'

'No, señor.'

'But a keen fisher of facts? And are you here, expecting to hook a great white shark rather than a minnow?' Perry asked as he sat.

'I'm not certain what I'm hoping to catch.'

'Won't that depend on the size of the hook and strength of the line?'

'And if I don't know either?'

'Then I'll be rude enough to suggest you might find a round of golf to be more productive.' He drank. 'Have you discovered who committed that terrible murder?'

'I'm afraid not.'

'So you want to know if we can help you any further than we did last time; which, basically, was not at all?'

'At the very least, you can answer one question.'

'Which is?'

'Did you know Señor Edward Gates?'

'Surely I said the last time you were here that I did not.'

'Would you like to change your answer?'

'What makes you think I might?'

'We asked the English police to give us as much information about Señor Gates as they could. Their report mentions a firm called Steadfast Security.'

Perry drank slowly. 'I think you have been trawling, not fishing with a single line.'

'Perhaps you would prefer to consider the matter and then have a word with me later at my office in Llueso?'

'You are a man of much tact.'

'Why d'you say that?' Iris asked sharply, no longer at ease.

'Unless I'm mistaken, the inspector is very kindly suggesting I might prefer to talk to him when you're not present because it would embarrass both of us if you were.' He turned to Alvarez. 'To make the situation quite clear – Yes, it probably was Gates who came here, but I did not meet him. I have made a full confession to my wife and she has somehow managed to forgive me.'

'You knew him in England?'

'I've never knowingly clapped eyes on him.'

'Will you tell me the facts?'

'Let me go back in time because, hopefully, it will present me in a slightly better light . . . I judge, inspector, that you have sufficient sympathetic understanding to know how emotion can sometimes empty a man's mind of all reason. Am I right?'

'Of much reason, yes.'

'But not all? If you've never suffered the total loss of all logical sanity, you are fortunate . . . The only thing pressing me was my own stupidity. But then the mind can usually imagine far worse than fact can deliver.' He drained his glass. 'I'm talking nonsense, which is a sign of nervousness. It's so much more difficult to bare one's soul than one's body . . . I need another drink. Please join me, inspector, so that the liquor which prompts my tongue will massage your ears.'

Alvarez finished his drink. Perry crossed to where his wife sat. 'A refill?' She shook her head. 'Would you rather leave us, darling?'

She reached up and gripped his wrist. 'No.'

He smiled at her. She released his wrist. He took Alvarez's glass, went through to the kitchen.

'It was very . . . difficult,' she said.

'I'm sure it was, señora.'

'It was as much my fault as his.' She abruptly spoke with much greater force. 'I never once stopped to think how it might seem to him.'

'You wouldn't have had to stop if I'd trusted you,' Perry shouted.

'That's not being fair to yourself,' she called back. She lowered her voice and spoke, without looking at Alvarez. 'You'll understand. I know you will.'

'I hope so, señora, but until I know what it is I have to understand, I can't be certain.'

Perry returned, handed Alvarez his glass, sat. He drank, held his glass just above his lap and stared at it. 'It began when we went to a cocktail party given by a couple whose choice of friends could hardly have been more eclectic.' He looked up and at Alvarez. 'We met Ivor Keen. We liked him sufficiently to pursue a friendship. Unfortunately . . . The long and the short of it is that after a while I began to think . . . "Think" has to be the wrong word, because if I'd stopped to think—'

She interrupted him. 'It was both our faults. For my part, I shouldn't have gone out with him when you were too busy to join in.'

148

'Why not? He was amusing company when I was so wrapped up in the business, I'd become a bore . . . There was no reason for suspicion, of course, until that goddamn voice in my head began to wonder why you were frequently going out with him and did you really go to the play or the opera or did you visit him in his flat? . . . Inside voices, inspector, don't have to shout to make themselves heard. Before long, I'd become convinced Iris was having an affair with Ivor. And in that madness, I decided to have her watched because, being in the process of selling my business very profitably, I decided that the moment I had confirmation that she was having an affair, I'd move all my money overseas and then face her with her adultery – that would make certain that no matter what financial settlement the court ordered on the breakdown of our marriage, their decision would be meaningless because she'd never be able to get her hands on a penny of mine. I'd had dealings with Steadfast Security, so I went to them and asked them to set up a surveillance on Iris. I'd sworn to love, comfort, and honour her – a great way of keeping my word!

'When I received their report, it said there was no evidence whatsoever to suggest she was having an affair with Keen even though they were frequently together. It will be difficult to understand how I longed to believe what I was being told, but just couldn't because of that vicious voice in my head. She'd been too clever for those who'd been watching her; she'd managed to throw sand in their eyes . . .

'I decided how I'd prove they were wrong. And if it sounds I was being . . .' He drank deeply. 'Let's use the word, contemptible. I told the security people I'd say to Iris I needed to be on my own for a while and so I'd take off on a solo sail. I believed that since they were having an affair, they'd never be able to resist making full use of my absence,

149

especially knowing I couldn't suddenly turn up and surprise them. The watchers would very soon have the proof.

'I sailed down the French coast, calling in at the little ports where one can still find traces of the old France. In Biarritz, I phoned my general manager to make certain the sale of the business was going smoothly and he told me that Iris kept asking if he knew where I was and how to get hold of me because she'd tried and tried to contact me on my mobile as well as on the yacht's radio, without success. Wondering what she wanted, I rang her at home. What she told me bowled me over. She was missing me more than she could have imagined possible, she was so miserable that Ivor had tried to get her to go out with him to cheer her up, but she wouldn't because she didn't think that would be fair to me when I was so far away, and couldn't I turn round and sail home? With that one conversation, my inner voice had its throat cut. Months of jealousy were blown away. I said she must get down to Biarritz as quickly as she could – I think I even suggested hiring a private plane—'

'You did,' she cut in, 'but I vetoed that idea, having Scots ancestry.'

He smiled. 'Anyway, I promised we'd have a voyage that would make up for everything – naturally without explaining it was my own contemptible behaviour that was meant by "everything".

'When we met . . . When one's been down in hell, the return becomes walking on air. And pretty soon I decided that if our marriage was to remain as golden as it had suddenly become once more, I had to confess to her what had been happening. It may be a cliché that total happiness demands total honesty, but that doesn't stop its being true. So I told her I'd been so certain she'd been having an affair with Ivor, I'd had her watched. Can you guess her response?'

'No, señor.'

'As tactful as ever! She laughed! Hadn't I ever realized that she'd been so at ease with Ivor, so ready to go out with him when I couldn't be with her, because he was gay? It was the final ironic twist – I couldn't have had less cause for jealousy.

'So life became truly golden for me . . .'

'For both of us,' she said quickly.

'For both of us,' he repeated. 'We sailed through the Straits of Gibraltar, decided to call in at Port Llueso for a few days because I'd always heard what a charming place it was. Almost immediately, Iris fell in love with the area and suggested we stay and find somewhere to live, at least for a while. If she'd asked for the moon, I'd have bought the shuttle. We rented a car, spoke to estate agents and found this house, which was available on an indeterminate lease because it was well away from the beaches and therefore not favoured by tourists.

'Not long ago – you'll know the date better than I! – Matilde told us in her strange and largely unintelligible Spanglish that someone had called and she'd told him to return another day. Naturally, I asked if he'd given a name and she said he had, but then came up with one that sounded about as unlikely as Pisistratus. As one does, we speculated who the caller might have been and eventually Iris suggested Ivor Keen, despite the total lack of similarity with the name Matilde had supplied. She'd told him over the phone before leaving England that she was joining me in Biarritz and was hoping to sail on; Keen then mentioned friends on this island with whom we ought to get in touch if we called here. She reckoned Ivor had come out and was staying with them and they'd mentioned we were living in this area – in fact, we had made contact with them, but it was far from a success; we'd little in common. Because of that, Ivor had come looking for us . . . That's why, the first time you came to the house and identified yourself, Iris suffered the sudden fear – totally illogical, but then much fear is – that you were going to tell her Ivor hadn't returned here because he'd been killed in an accident.

'Then you said you were trying to identify the unknown Englishman and that gave Iris fresh worry – was Ivor alive, but in some sort of trouble? That fear disappeared to be replaced by yet another when you told me that the dead man had been identified. I'd never met Gates, but had been told he would be in field-charge of my case. Iris, knowing how much I'd hate admitting to anyone else how I'd suspected her, was shocked to hear the name and I hastily made up that ridiculous story of her cousin . . . Of course, life usually playing the joker, I've ended up having to admit the truth anyway. Have I made sense?'

'Indeed, señor. Thank you for being so frank.'

'I don't suppose . . .' Perry became silent.

'I will make certain that all you have told me will be treated as strictly confidential.'

'You are . . .' He stopped again, seeking the right words.

'Very, very kind,' she said.

Alvarez stood. His job so often caused distress, fear, anger, that when it occasioned a warm response, he felt as if he'd added a little good to the world. But then he was rather sentimental.

Seventeen

'Was he telling the truth when he said Gates did not return to the house?' Fuster asked.

Alvarez, who'd been left to stand, moved the chair in front of the desk and sat. 'What reason could he have for lying?'

'To be able to deny he was ever presented with the bill Gates had brought.'

'Would a wealthy man bother?'

'The rich always avoid paying when they can; that's why they're rich.'

'Perhaps you reckon he murdered Gates in the hopes that the bill wouldn't be presented a second time by someone else?'

'I always distinguish between possibility and absurdity . . . The report from Steadfast Security which Gates had brought out from England was never found, was it?'

'It must have disappeared when his hotel room was stripped of all personal belongings to try to prevent identification.'

'You don't think everything might have been taken in order to make it seem the report was not the specific object of the clearance?'

'Since Perry had confessed everything to his wife, why should he be so concerned by a report which merely confirmed what she already knew?'

'But did she? Might he not have lied to you and in fact told her nothing?'

'In that case, surely he'd have taken the opportunity to speak to me here, when he could make certain his wife wouldn't hear him?'

'I am not suggesting he now be considered a suspect.'

'That surely is what you've been inferring?'

'An inference lies in the mind of the listener, not the speaker . . . Nevertheless, there has to be the possibility that prior to your visit today, he had confessed nothing to her.'

'You imagine that if that were the case, she would have just calmly sat there, silent, while she learned that he'd been so convinced she'd been screwing around, he'd had her watched?'

'A wife should always support her husband's honour.'

'I'd guess Señora Perry is post-lib. Hearing that news for the first time would have provoked a tumble of four-letter words.'

'Not if well brought up.'

'For the English, such words have become a sign of equality breeding. She was not hearing anything for the first time. He'd confessed everything, she'd forgiven and perhaps come to love him a little more because he'd shown such jealousy.'

'A ridiculous suggestion!'

'Human nature can be a lot odder than most people think possible.'

'Sitting here as I am, I have no quarrel with that proposition . . . Did you question Munar again?'

'He wasn't at Ca'n Portens.'

'You have great difficulty in finding people at home.'

'No more than in finding them not at home . . . But the visit may have paid off handsomely.'

'In what way?'

'I had a chat with Luisa Munar and she let slip something interesting. When Gates called there that Wednesday evening, she says a third person was present.'

'Of course. She has repeatedly claimed she was there.'

'I'm afraid I'm not very pedantic. I should have said a fourth person. Angel Gomilio Balle was also there. Why haven't we been told this before? A hundred to one, because Gomilio has previously been identified as a member of the smuggling gang and so, had his presence been known, it would have been obvious the two of them were organizing the reception and hiding of the consignment being landed.'

'Has it occurred to you to speak to the Guardia to ask if Gomilio's name is known?'

'It's occurred, but there's not yet been the time.'

'A good detective makes the time.'

'It's odd you should say that. One of Salas's favourite sayings.'

'He is a man of great sagacity.'

'And the modesty frequently to conceal that fact.'

'You do yourself no credit when you make an ambiguous remark such as that.'

'It's the listener, not the speaker, who identifies ambiguity.'

'I understand ever more clearly why provocation sometimes overcomes the superior chief's natural discretion . . . Ring the Guardia now. And if their answer is in the affirmative, question Gomilio this afternoon.'

'If I find him at home.'

Sa Setri was a small village on the mountainous north coast where rock often plunged precipitously into the sea. In the summer, many artists stayed or visited there for the pleasure of the evenings when a golden sun sank below the horizon to turn the waters red or nights when the moon sent a shaft of shimmering light across the darkened sea; in the winter, when gales lashed a frenzied assault on the rock, artists found their inspiration in the bars in the cities.

For some reason for which no one could readily account, the village had always been a haven for smugglers and as late as the early twentieth century there had been a battle between them and the Guardia which had left one dead, two seriously injured, and thousands of dumped cigarettes sodden and useless. There were some uncharitable enough to suggest that the many days of mourning had concerned more the cigarettes than the dead man.

The last house in Carrer Infanta Paz stood on the highest village ground and a light on the roof could be seen for many kilometres out to sea. Alvarez stepped into the front room, so barely furnished as almost to be unfurnished, and called out. An old woman, in black, shuffled in and stared at him with eyes sharper than she would have wished.

'I'm looking for Angel,' he said.

She was silent.

'Is he here?'

Her silence continued.

'I'm in no hurry, so take your time.'

'Who are you?' she asked, with the voice of a corn-crake.

'Cuerpo General de Policia.'

She began to munch her toothless gums together.

'Is he here?'

'No.'

'Where will I find him?'

'Anywhere.'

'Except here? When will he be back?'

'Can't say.'

A canary sang in snatches. Outside, a Mobylette went past, its exhaust magnified because the silencer had been removed by the rider who liked to imagine himself seated on a Suzuki TR750.

As the minutes passed, the woman became increasingly uneasy and her munching rate increased. Then, from overhead, came the sounds of movement and, a moment later, a shout. 'Who was it?'

She stared at the floor.

They heard descending footsteps. A man, short in height but very broad of shoulder, entered; his face, when not concealed by a bushy beard, bore the mark of sun and sea and suggested a contempt of fear, perhaps even of death. He came to an abrupt stop. 'Who are you?' he demanded roughly.

She answered. 'An inspector in the Cuerpo.'

'Are you Angel Gomilio?' Alvarez asked.

'What if I am?'

'I want the answers to some questions.'

'Why?'

'I'm investigating a murder.'

Gomilio shrugged his shoulders.

'Aren't you interested in knowing who's been murdered?'

'No.'

'An Englishman, name of Gates. His head and hands were cut off.'

'Pity it doesn't happen more often.'

'If it did, tourists would stop coming to the island and your trade would suffer badly.'

'People would still want fish.'

'But not Glen Grant-Glenlivet whisky and Bisquit Dubouche cognac.'

Gomilio stared at him, surprise quickly giving way to anger. He clenched his large fists.

'You and Miguel Munar work together.'

'Don't work with no one.'

'The Guardia reckon you two make a couple.'

'The Guardia!' He cleared his throat, spat.

'The two of you were busy at the beginning of last month.'

'I don't know no Munar.'

The old woman said: 'Why are you—'

'Shut your trap,' Gomilio said fiercely. 'Clear out.'

Showing no concern at his loutish behaviour, she shuffled out of the room and closed the door behind herself.

'Where are you from?' Gomilio demanded.

'Llueso.'

'Then this ain't your patch.'

'Inspector Fuster asked me to help him.'

'Smuggling ain't the Cuerpo's business.'

'Did I actually mention smuggling?'

Gomilio's expression suggested it was costing him great effort to keep his temper in check.

'Of course, you are quite right; normally, smuggling is not our pigeon. But all the signs are that it played a part in the murder which means we become involved. So now you can tell me what happened at Miguel's finca when you were there last month.'

'I don't know no Munar. That Wednesday I was here and the old woman will swear to that.'

'As, no doubt, will several other people because they're paid to or are afraid what will happen to them if they don't. Interesting you should have mentioned Wednesday.'

'What's so bleeding interesting about it?'

'I didn't mention the date or day. But it was a Wednesday. Coincidence? Much more likely, of course, that you knew which day you needed to cover.'

Gomilio swore.

'Let's sort things out. I know you and Miguel were at

Ca'n Portens that Wednesday, getting ready to receive the cargo landed in Cala Balera. An Englishman turned up in a car, wanting to know where Perry lived. He saw you both and that set the alarm bells ringing because if the Guardia learned the two of you had been together, they'd be convinced Miguel was, as suspected, in the smuggling racket and he was providing storage. As a consequence, they'd search his property like they were looking for diamonds and quite possibly find the cave being used. What I don't know is what happened next.'

'I wasn't there, I don't know no Munar,' Gomilio said violently.

'There are two possible reasons for your lying. You're not prepared to admit you were at the finca simply because that will finger you and Miguel; or you're afraid it will provide the motive for your murder of the Englishman, Gates.'

'I wasn't there.'

'You're not stupid, so you know as well as me the practical difference between smuggling and murder. Smuggling's the result of taxation and the only people it really hurts are the tax collectors and who gives a damn if they're in pain? But murder frightens because it destroys the innocent. So someone who wouldn't think twice of swearing by all his ancestors that on that Wednesday you were sitting in this house, weaving, will refuse to lie when it becomes a case of murder. The more you go on denying the obvious, the more I'll reckon you've reason not to see sense. Perhaps the shock of finding a foolproof scheme blow up in your face after having cut off head and hands to prevent identification.'

There was a long silence.

'The longer you deny knowing Miguel, the better the word "murderer" seems to fit you.'

'I ain't ever met him or been near his finca. And if you

159

reckon you can scare me into saying I have, you need a fresh pair of cojones.'

'The older one becomes, the more one wishes that were possible.'

Alvarez left. He had no doubt Gomilio would be hoping that when he stepped out of the doorway, it would take him into the path of a speeding car.

'It sounds,' Fuster said in his most pretentious manner, 'as if you made a complete hash of questioning Gomilio. You let him understand our position without learning from him anything of consequence.'

'We now know he refuses to admit he was at Ca'n Portens.'

'A negative with negative value.'

'Why is he denying that when it must be obvious to him we know he's lying? Certainly, he had a motive. And yet . . .'

'Well?'

'Would someone who's always preferred to do rather than to plan appreciate the need to go to Hotel Platjador after the murder and clear Gates's room of everything personal to try to prevent an investigation?'

'I remember your dismissing the possibility that Perello was the murderer on those same grounds.'

'Character is so often the key to a solution.'

'The character of the criminal or the investigator? . . . . You say Gomilio has an alibi?'

'If called upon to provide one, he will have.'

'Faked?'

'Of course.'

'Then did you not challenge him to provide one in order to prove he's a liar?'

'I judged it best not to do so for the moment.'

'On what grounds?'

'He'll be very busy setting one up.'

'To most, that would seem to provide every reason for forestalling him.'

'The more careful he tries to be, the more complicated his alibi will become. He'll call on several people to support him and when there are many, there is always a weak link.'

'A doubtful, even reckless thesis . . . What car does he own?'

'There's not been time to check that out.'

'A good investigator—'

'Works twenty-six hours a day and dies young.'

'You need not fear doing that. Find out what car he owns and whether that, or Munar's, was seen during the relevant times near where the body was found.'

'The area is not exactly teeming with people who might have seen it.'

'Neither is it empty of them.'

'What I'm trying to say is—'

'Obvious.'

'You're talking about Miguel's car as well as Gomilio's. Are you seriously suspecting Miguel?'

'He has a motive.'

'You no longer regard Perello as a suspect?'

'I am close to arresting him.'

'Then why waste time and effort over Gomilio and Miguel?'

'Until a case is closed, all possibilities must be followed.'

'Even when you're convinced that that's pointless and results have to be negative? Didn't you say negatives have negative values?'

'Some can have positive values.'

'It sounds as complicated as the new maths.' He turned and left.

*   *   *

As Jaime pushed the bottle of brandy across the dining-room table, Alvarez sniffed the air. 'Maybe she's cooking something special.' He picked up the bottle and poured himself a drink.

'She's in a cheerful mood.'

'Then we may be lucky.'

'She was singing a while back.'

'Just so long as the song wasn't about an innocent woman left holding the baby by a heartless man.' Alvarez added four cubes of ice to the brandy.

'With her,' Jaime said in aggrieved tones, 'it's always the man's fault.'

'Women carefully forget who ate the first fruit.'

'Fruit? Ate the first fruit? There are times when even you don't seem to know what the hell you're talking about.'

'That's roughly what Fuster said earlier on.'

'The inspector from Barcelona? The only thing people from there know about is money – other people's.'

They drank.

The bead curtain parted and Dolores stepped into the room. Her hair was dishevelled, her face flushed and damp, her frock stained under the armpits by sweat, her apron askew, yet still her air was one of haughty superiority. 'You're here, Enrique.'

Her tone had not been unduly aggressive, yet he decided an apology might be sensible. 'I'm sorry I'm late, but Fuster held me up.'

'That doesn't matter. I was worried because the meal can't wait.'

'What are we having?'

'Capó al Rei Jaume.'

'My favourite!'

'You say many things are your favourite.'

'Because everything you cook is perfect.'

'An absurdity!' She was smiling when she returned into the kitchen.

'You do lay it on with a trowel,' Jaime muttered.

'Where's the harm if it keeps her happy?'

'It makes her big-headed.'

There was a call from the kitchen. 'So who is big-headed?'

Jaime looked very nervously at the bead curtain. Alvarez waited for him to provide an answer that would satisfy Dolores and then, when clearly this was not going to happen, said loudly: 'Magdalena. Some man's told her she looks like the young Grace Kelly and she believes that.'

'When her eyes are so far apart they are almost alongside her ears and her nose is so long it barely misses her mouth? Whoever told her that was hoping to confuse her small mind with ridiculous words. Men were ever deceivers.'

'But who ate the first fruit?' Jaime called out.

She put her head through the bead curtain. 'What fruit?'

'Ask Enrique.'

'Why?'

'He knows what it was.'

'And you obviously don't. Why talk about things that escape your understanding?' Her tone remained pleasant. 'The meal will be ready in ten minutes so call the children and remind them to make certain they wash their hands and faces.' She withdrew her head.

Jaime drank. 'Why didn't you tell me if it was oranges or lemons or whatever?' he asked Alvarez.

'I didn't think you'd be daft enough to say what you did to her.'

'I reckon you can't get dafter than talk about fruit when you don't seem to know what it is.'

'I'm inclined to agree.'

Dolores called out: 'Have you told the children to come in?'

Alvarez drained his glass. Since Dolores was cooking an ambrosian dish, it behove one of them to sacrifice a little drinking time. He stood, went through to the road to call Isabel and Juan indoors.

The phone rang as Dolores served Jaime a second portion of capon stuffed with sweet potato, apple, sobrassada, raisins, egg, bread, milk, and sweet paprika. She passed the plate across and, as the phone continued to ring, looked at the two men, sighed, left the table and walked through to the front room.

The minutes passed. Jaime said: 'I reckon women spend half their lives talking on the phone. What did they do when there weren't any?'

'Pretended to listen to their husbands.' Alvarez refilled his glass with wine.

Juan ate his last mouthful. 'What's for afters?'

'How would we know?' Jaime answered.

'I want it quickly so I can go back and play some more with Pedro.'

'Then tell your mother that. And say we're all waiting.'

Juan did not move.

'You're too scared!' Isabel said scornfully.

'No, I'm not.'

'Then go and tell her.'

Juan stood, hesitated, saw Isabel's smile broaden, and went through to the front room. They heard him mumble something.

'Then they'll have to go on waiting.' Dolores's voice was loud, clear, and aggressive. 'The apple pie on the kitchen table? That's for Eulalia whose mother is very ill so she has not time to cook . . . Anyone who can't wait just for a little while can eat bread . . . Then you're not hungry.'

'Mummy sounds annoyed,' Isabel remarked.

'And now tell us it's sunny outside,' Jaime muttered.

Juan returned to the dining-room, his expression sullen.

'Who's she talking to?' Jaime asked.

'I don't know. And why can't I have some apple pie?'

'Because it's your fault,' Isabel said.

'You're not going to get any either.'

'I don't want any.'

'Liar. Stupid liar.'

'Clear out both of you or I'll learn you some manners,' Jaime snapped.

As Isabel and Juan left, Dolores came through the doorway. 'I am told you are waiting impatiently?' Her words were encased in ice. She sat and ate three mouthfuls, then said, 'Perhaps all men enjoy inflicting pain which is why there are wars. They like to strut around with their medals and laugh at the women who worry because their children starve.'

'What's got you talking like this?' Jaime asked.

'You do not understand? . . . But how naive of me! If you drown your wits in alcohol, how can you be expected to understand the simplest thing?'

'Steady on.'

She ate a piece of chicken. 'I have had to learn.' She put knife and fork down on the plate. 'Sweet Mary and how I have had to learn! A woman sacrifices her whole life to provide a perfect home for a man and his thanks are to treat her with contempt. Let her ask for one small favour and even if he promises it, he'll not carry it out because he's happy to cause her the pain of his failure. Ayee! If there were a medicine to cure such pain as I feel, I would drink it as you swill the wine.'

'I've had hardly any this meal . . .'

'A woman has to learn. She may believe that one day a

man will cease to be completely selfish, indifferent to anyone but himself, but eventually she discovers her stupidity.
Nothing will change him. And therefore there is reason for
doing nothing. That must be true. So I will no longer spend
more hours than there are in the day in a kitchen hotter then
the Sahara, preparing meals that will be guzzled without a
thought of all they have cost me. I will continue to put food
on the table, yes; as a wife, that remains my duty and unlike a
man, I will always honour it. But duty does not mean luxury
and the food will be simple; very simple.' She stood, an
Amazon queen, surveying her cowed enemies.

'What have I done this time? Jaime asked miserably.

'As is usual, you have done nothing.'

'Then why go on at me so?'

'Did I once mention you?'

'If it's not me, who are you bellyaching at?'

'Perhaps Enrique will be able to answer you. It is just
possible my words might have pierced his indifference to
another's suffering.'

Alvarez leaned across, opened the nearer sideboard door,
and, much to Jaime's shocked surprise, brought out a bottle
of brandy. Dolores's expression darkened and became posi-
tively threatening as he poured himself a drink, then pushed
the bottle across the table. Jaime shook his head vigorously
to make certain she noticed.

'I guess that phone call was from Luisa?' Alvarez said.

'Yes,' she replied curtly.

'And there's trouble?'

'Trouble enough even to meet your desires.'

'Exactly what's happened?'

'Someone rang Miguel. Afterwards, he swore he'd kill
Luisa for betraying him. She kept telling him she'd only
been trying to help but, like any man, he refused to listen.

Now she is in tears because of you. You, who were asked to help her.'

'And landed in the pozo negro as a consequence.'

'And this is how you gain your revenge? Let a woman be overwhelmed by trouble and a man laughs; let a man be but disturbed and he revenges himself on a woman . . .'

'You're talking nonsense.'

She was so surprised, she could not immediately reply.

'I had to make the inquiries I did. If these caused trouble for Miguel, that's unfortunate. But it's his responsibility, not mine.'

She tried to regain the initiative. 'You didn't care what the consequences were . . .'

'I couldn't.'

'Only a man—'

'Because for him it has become a murder case.'

She drew in her breath with an audible hiss. 'Murder . . . But I'm talking about Miguel, Luisa's husband.'

'So am I.'

'Mother of God! You can't be suggesting . . .'

'Luisa told me something so important it had to be followed up, whatever the consequences. And because of what I learned, Miguel has to be under suspicion.'

She stared at him for several seconds. Then she turned and walked into the kitchen.

Jaime reached for the brandy and poured himself a drink. 'You shouldn't have spoken like that,' he whispered. 'God knows what will happen now! Life will be hell for everyone for weeks and weeks.'

Alvarez accepted that his choice of words had been injudicious, that he would not have spoken them had he given any thought to what he was about to say; but her irrational accusations had angered him . . .

The bead curtain swished as she returned to stand facing them, arms folded across her chest.

The two men mentally braced themselves.

'I'm sorry, Enrique,' she said humbly. 'I should have understood.' She returned to the kitchen.

'I don't believe it,' Jaime muttered. 'I don't bloody believe it. Apologizing!' He drank. 'Know what? Next time she starts going on at me, I'll shut her up by telling her she's talking nonsense.' But he didn't believe that either.

Eighteen

The room was very stuffy and Alvarez felt sweat gather across his shoulders and under his armpits. He looked resentfully at the fan, an old one, which refused to work at its fastest speed. Now he was denied his old room, he remembered it as offering the comfort of an air-conditioned lounge . . . Until the case was solved, Fuster would remain in command, in Llueso, in his room. Truly, man was made to suffer. Indeed, only that morning, he'd deemed it wise to cut short his merienda in case his prolonged absence was noted. The case had to be solved quickly so that Fuster left and life returned to normal. But was a solution even in distant sight?

There were motiveless murders, but this was not one; here, there had clearly been a very strong motive. Who had had direct or indirect contact with Gates; of them, who could have had reason to kill him?

Perry. He had engaged Steadfast Security to investigate the possibility (certainty, he had thought at the time) of his wife's infidelity. He claimed never to have met Gates. There was no obvious reason for disbelieving him, but there had to be the possibility this was said in order to distance himself from any suspicion – even if there were no immediate cause for anyone to be suspicious of him. Turn things round to obtain a different perspective – if it could be shown it was most unlikely he had ever met Gates, his veracity would be greatly strengthened.

Alvarez asked the woman in charge of Reference at the Cuerpo to try and find out the telephone number of Steadfast Security in England – address not known, but possibly the firm was based near Peters Green. She surprised him by saying that on such indefinite information, the task might prove difficult, but she'd do her best. She surprised him even more when fifteen minutes later she rang back and gave him the number.

He dialled this and when the connexion was made, introduced himself, was about to explain the reason for the call to the young woman when she interrupted him.

'What's the weather like with you?'

'Very sunny, señorita.'

'It's raining here.'

'I am sorry to hear that. I'm phoning because—'

'Is it warm?'

'Far too hot.'

'Is the sea warm?'

'I expect so.'

'D'you mean, you don't go swimming?'

'I am too busy . . .'

'I'd be in the water all day.'

'Not if you had to work as hard as I do, señorita. I should like to speak to someone who handled the case concerning Señor Perry.'

'I'm going to Crete next month for my holiday. Do you think it will be hot there?'

'So hot you will long to return to the cool of England.'

'Never! . . . I'll put you through to Mr Pearson.'

After a brief pause, a man said: 'Pearson speaking. Is it correct that you are a detective in Majorca?'

'Yes, señor. And my call is in connexion with the murder of Señor Gates.'

'A dreadful affair. Are you close to making an arrest?'

Spanish honour must be upheld. 'We are reasonably certain we have identified the murderer, but as you will understand, we now have to find the necessary proof to take the case to court.'

'Yes, of course. So often the hardest part. I must say, you speak good English.'

'Thank you.'

'I can never understand why so few foreigners do – makes it difficult to exchange views and ideas . . . Well, how can I help?'

'We need to be certain if Señor Perry would have known Señor Gates; would have ever actually met him?'

'Unless there's good reason for a client to identify an operative, in certain cases we take care that he does not; obviously, if during a surveillance a client inadvertently indicates he recognizes the operative, the party may well latch on to what's happening. In fact, Mr Perry wanted to meet our main operative and became quite annoyed when I said that was very inadvisable. I gained the impression that he wished to tell Gates how to conduct the case. Of course, very successful men often think they're omniscient as well as omnipotent and having lost their sense of humour, can't see the funny side of that. Frankly, Mr Perry must be a difficult man to live with – as proved by his suspicious nature – and he's very lucky to have a wife as loyal and forgiving as Mrs Perry has proved herself to be.'

'Then Señor Perry never did meet Señor Gates?'

'As I've been saying, no, he didn't.'

But previously, he'd never actually said that. Alvarez thanked the other, rang off.

He settled back in the chair. It surely was reasonable to assume Gates had called at Ca'n Portens on the Wednesday evening; on the Thursday, Matilde had told him the Perrys were away on their yacht. He had intended to deliver two things, the case report and the firm's account. The report confirmed what Perry had already learned – his wife was not unfaithful. It was the messenger with bad news who had risked death when he delivered it, not the bringer of good news.

Miguel. Gates had seen him in the company of another man, Gomilio. Had authority known that, they would have deduced Miguel's finca was probably the hiding place for newly landed contraband and would have organized a search sufficiently thorough to uncover the cave, no matter how well concealed its entrance. Miguel would have been convicted and sent to jail. But why would Gates ever have considered the sighting of the two men at Ca'n Portens to be of any consequence whatsoever? In what circumstances would he, a foreigner on holiday, be likely to pass on that information to the police?

Gomilio. With one proviso, the same questions and doubts arose. He was a man of strong passions and if he had thought there was even a chance in a hundred Gates might alert authority, he would have been prepared to reduce those odds to zero. But how would he have known where Gates was staying?

Perello. Largely an unknown character in so far as he – Alvarez – was concerned. Natalia said he was very far from bright. It had taken him a long time to realize Lucía was sleeping around. When he had finally understood, he had become so angrily jealous, he had hit her. Jealousy was a frequent motive for murder and in a mind less balanced than normal, it could have become an overwhelming one. But would, could, he have had the forethought to empty the bedroom of Gates's personal belongings? Or should Natalia's judgment not be accepted uncritically because her basis for it was specific – Perello's relationship with Lucía – rather than general? Alvarez sighed. He was going to have to find the answers to many questions . . . To cheer himself up, he reached down for the bottle of brandy in the bottom right-hand drawer of the desk, only to be reminded there was neither drawer nor bottle.

Cala Roig, once no more than a few fishermen's homes, had slowly become a small, attractive resort surrounding a double, north-facing bay whose waters were crystal clear and in which a considerable variety of marine life existed – once even a two-metre sea snake, according to one swimmer, but that was generally credited to the strength of the drinks served at the bars before the owners had learned the full benefits of charging more for less. Then, abruptly, the pace of development had increased and now Cala Roig was just one more jumble of housing, hotels, bars, and memento shops whose goods well suited those who bought them.

Five generations of the Perello family had lived in the small, stone-built house with land of almost a hectare, set two hundred metres back from the water. Two of the men had died at sea fifty-three years previously when their open boat had been caught in a sudden autumn storm and a small stone memorial – set in the poorest soil because sentiment was to be admired, but fruit and vegetables were essential – still marked their passing.

Ana, a small and seemingly frail woman, had been born at the western end of the island. A widow for twenty-one years – her husband had died from a heart attack – she gained much solace from the fact that he had not seen the worst of the development. She would remember when he had sat outside on an old wooden chair with their first born on his knee – she had died when two; life was sometimes unbearable, yet it had to be borne – and he had told the uncomprehending child how God had decided to build the most beautiful place on earth and had dug out the earth and the rocks with His hands and used this spoil to build the jagged mountains which fashioned the bay. It was because of these memories that, many years before, she had first refused to sell the property to developers. Friends had called her a fool; then praised her cunning as land values increased beyond a sane person's imagination. There had been several more offers at different times and the last one had mentioned so many millions of pesetas it was as if they were but thousands; three of her four surviving children had urged her to sell, their minds already filled with images of new cars and larger homes, but Emilio had begged her to keep the property because it was his bolt-hole from the outside, often hostile world . . .

'The others, they say sell; Emilio says don't sell.' Ana scratched her nose. 'The pesetas have never worried him.'

Then he was an unusual man, Alvarez thought. And lucky, to live in a small corner of heaven. The land rose up quite steeply from the water, so that from where they sat, in the shade of the house, they could look out at the bay, their eyes shielded from much of the ugly development. He wondered for how long she would be able to resist the pressure to sell? He knew several families where the parents had finally given in to their children's demands. In years past, no son or daughter would have urged a parent to leave the family home; in years past, no finca had been worth many, many millions to the foreigners or the developers who knew not the true value of anything.

'What do you want with him?' Ana asked, her voice now sharp.

The cat defending her kitten with tooth and claw. 'To have a chat.'

'Like the other inspector? He frightened Emilio.'

'I'm not surprised. Fuster says things that frighten me.'

174

'He keeps accusing Emilio of killing the Englishman. Is he stupid?'

'There are those who might say so.'

'My Emilio never hurt anyone; never – do you understand?'

'I am here to try and understand.'

She spoke more calmly. 'How?'

'I want to talk to Emilio and learn the kind of person he is. Then I will be more certain what is true and what is untrue.'

'I have told the other inspector the truth again and again. Yet always he calls me a liar.'

'He finds it difficult to believe anyone but himself.'

'He keeps asking Emilio where he was. I tell him, Emilio was with me. Yet he will not believe.'

'Unfortunately, like a wife, a mother does not make a good witness for her son. She is always ready to lie for him.'

'What else would you expect a mother to do?'

She seemed unaware of the inference of what she had just said.

'Tell me about Lucía.'

'A woman who lacks shame!'

'Isn't that being a bit hard on her?'

'He told me he wanted to bring her here. A mother needs to meet the woman her son is accompanying. She came here. She was dressed as not even a puta would dress when I was young; there are sights only a husband should see. She looked around this house and saw no fine furniture on which people waste their money these days, and inside she was jeering at me – I swear to that – because I wore grey. The likes of her don't wear black even on the day of burial. But when he showed her what was our land, her eyes became hungry. After she had gone, I told Emilio, she likes not you, but the money the land would make. He was very angry. He said many things no mother should have to listen to. Because he is my son, I have forgotten them, but they still hurt.'

'If he's fond of her, you can't blame him too much for being upset by what you said.'

'I spoke the truth. A man uses a puta, he should not be fond of her. Is a mother not to guide her son's future? Married to her, he would own a bed that other men wore out.'

'Does he want to marry her?'

She fidgeted with a button on the front of her grey cotton dress. In her face there was pride, pain, and fear. 'His father, may God be kind to him, used to say to me, Emilio is not like the others. I argued and replied, it just takes him longer to do things. A mother can hide her eyes to almost anything. But his father was right. And Emilio believes what others tell him. When that puta whispers sweet words, he cannot understand she is secretly laughing because he believes her.'

'But he did discover she was very friendly with another man and that made him hit her.'

'But not angry enough, nor did he hit her hard enough; when she told him she'd been stupid, but would never be stupid again, he believed what she said.'

'You think he really did believe her?'

'Have I not just told you he cannot understand she has nothing but contempt for him because he will not understand she is a lying puta?'

'Have you said all this to Inspector Fuster?'

'You think I would tell him that my Emilio . . .' She did not finish.

'It might help the inspector understand.'

'That man can understand nothing.'

He stared out at the bay. She was right. Fuster would look

out, as he was doing, and see only water, mountains, and sky; the heart-plucking beauty would escape him. 'Where is Emilio now?'

'Why do you ask?'

'I need to speak with him.'

'I don't know where he is.'

'Is that the truth?'

'You call me a liar?' she demanded fiercely.

'You have told me, a mother will lie to the devil if needs be.'

'Perhaps. But truly I do not know. Perhaps he is with the puta.'

'When he returns, tell him I want to help and therefore he should come to the post and talk to me.'

'You are going to arrest him!' Her voice became high from fear.

'Of course not. But I have to understand things which only he can explain . . . When Inspector Fuster speaks, it is as a Catalan; when I speak, it is as a Mallorquin.'

She said slowly: 'The other inspector is a man who likes to bring fear; you like to ease pain. I will tell Emilio to see you.'

As he was sitting at the desk, wondering why time slowed when one was hot, thirsty, and tired, Fuster stepped into the room. 'As busy as ever!'

'A moment's thought can be more valuable than an hour's action.'

'You will be relieved to learn that neither thought nor action is required of you. The case is complete.'

'It's what?'

'Earlier, I was informed Perello was here, at the post, asking to speak to the inspector. You will understand what that means.'

'Yes, he wants—'

'Guilt motivates in different ways. One man will laugh at it, a second will ignore it, a third will find it so oppressive that he has to relieve himself of its burden. Do you follow what I'm saying?'

'Some feel guilty, some don't.'

'It was clear that Perello was driven here by—'

'A car?'

'Must you indulge in juvenile humour?'

'Are you about to claim that it was his guilt which forced him here? If so, you couldn't be more wrong. He came to prove he had nothing to do with Gates's death.'

'You have questioned him at length?'

'Not at all.'

'I have.'

'You don't think we should start working together?'

'There can be very little, if any, point in our doing so. Having questioned him, I can say without fear of contradiction that he murdered Gates.'

'Then you haven't talked to his mother?'

'Have you?'

'Yes.'

'You should not have questioned her without my express instructions to do so.'

'Don't forget to enter my malfeasance in your crime diary.'

'The facts will be noted.'

Alvarez made an effort to promote a happier atmosphere. 'Look, however we regard each other, let's work together for the good of the investigation. I've spoken to his mother and—'

'An unnecessary exercise. Perello thinks he is in love with the woman, Lucía, and he exposed the extent of his angry jealousy when he assaulted her. He has no alibi for

the window of time during which the murder was almost
certainly committed—'

'His mother swears he was with her.'

'Only a neophyte will give any weight to her words.'

'I accept that, but there always has to be the chance she
could be telling the truth.'

'She isn't.'

'How can you be certain?'

'The cigarette lighter.'

'What cigarette lighter?'

'Before making the many wild statements you have, it
would have been to your advantage to acquaint yourself
with all the facts of the case.'

'Somewhat difficult when some have deliberately been
kept from me.'

'The superior chief gave me some advice before I took
command here. If I hoped to conduct the investigation
in a logical, comprehensible manner, I should make certain you handled only those aspects of it where incompetence would not be disastrous. Since the facts are now
incontrovertible, there seems no reason for you not to be
told them. When Perello came here, he was searched; on
his person was a silver cigarette lighter on which were
engraved the letters RTG. The probability that this had
belonged to Gates was obvious, but as I never leap to
conclusions—'

'Did Perello explain how he got hold of Gates's lighter?'

'Should you not first determine whether this was confirmed as having belonged to Gates?'

'I took that as read.'

'To take anything as read in a case such as this suggests
either mental sclerosis or mental laziness . . . Naturally, I
immediately got in touch with England and asked them to
make inquiries. With highly commendable rapidity, they

have informed me that Gates's parents gave him the lighter on his twenty-first birthday.'

'You sent a photograph and not just a description to make a positive identification?'

Fuster's lips tightened. 'Having identified the owner of the lighter, I asked Perello how he came into possession of it. He refused to answer.'

'Why did he refuse?'

'That is not obvious?'

'No.'

'In Barcelona we say, "A man can look at a book, but that does not mean he can read."'

'In Mallorca, we say, "A man can read a book without understanding what it's about."'

'I have arrested Perello for the murder of Gates.'

'Ridiculous!'

'Your judgment justifies my action.'

'This case is about character as much as anything.'

'You are referring to the characters of those investigating?'

'Of those being investigated.'

'An assessment of character is of more validity than the facts?'

'Of the supposed facts, yes.'

'Presumably, you are a prime exponent of the belief that it is entropy which drives the world . . . Perello, seeing his slut of a woman going out with another man, became insanely jealous – we have the evidence of his assault. He killed Gates and tried to make identification of the body impossible, yet was so dazzled by the silver cigarette lighter that he stole it from the corpse. He forced his mother to try to provide him with an alibi, but then could not overcome the cancer of guilt. That has been eating into his mind until he came here earlier, seeking redemption through confession . . .'

'Has he confessed?'

'Not yet.'

'But you claim he was seeking redemption through con-fession?'

'Guilt provokes yet at the same time muzzles.'

'I'm in danger of becoming dizzy . . . Look, guilt has nothing to do with his coming here and it wasn't you he wanted to speak to. I told his mother to send him along so I could have a chat with him.'

'Then undoubtedly it was as well that the duty cabo directed him to me rather than waiting for your return from wherever you were or by now confusion would be complete.' He turned and left the room.

Dolores said: 'Antonia phoned me earlier on.'

Alvarez ate another spoonful of aroz brut. He couldn't be certain which of the many Antonias they knew she was referring to, but her manner made it obvious the phone call spelt trouble for someone.

She looked across at Juan. 'Stop fidgeting.'

'I wasn't,' Juan objected.

'If I say you were, you were.'

The sense of gloom became general.

'Antonia has been speaking to Ana. She says Ana is so distraught, the doctor had to give her a sedative.'

Jaime was reaching for the bottle of wine when he realized she was looking at him; he picked up the salt cellar.

'I have seasoned the dish.'

He hastily put the salt cellar down.

'Poor Ana! To have suffered so much. Her daughter died when so young and her husband before he became old. She has struggled and struggled for her family that is left and what has been her reward? Three of her children worry her to sell the house and land and will not understand she wishes to stay there because that is where she has lived ever since

181

her marriage; that it is where her daughter and her husband lay before they were buried. Of course, one should not be surprised by her children. Has there ever been a man capable of appreciating an emotion that does not concern himself? And as if that were not enough, there is now Emilio.'

'Are you talking about Emilio Perello's mother?' Alvarez asked.

'You would like me to think you did not know that?'

'I had no idea what her Christian name is. Look, if she's been complaining—'

'When a woman's trust is broken, she does not complain, because life has taught her the uselessness of that; but when on her own, she weeps a little because it is hard to learn again that men have no understanding or compassion.'

'It wasn't my fault that—'

'Or the courage to admit to their heartless lies.'

'When I asked her to come to the post so I could talk to Emilio, it never occurred to me he'd just ask for the inspector and so be taken to Fuster, who has such a complicated mind he believes it was guilt which drove Emilio to the post because he longed to be punished to redeem his conscience.'

'I don't understand,' Jaime said.

'In order to do so,' she said tartly, 'you would have to be capable of believing you will help an elderly widow enjoy life by making it unbearably miserable.'

Nineteen

As Isabel carried the last plates out to the kitchen, Alvarez stood. 'I'm going out.'

Jaime, his hands on the bottle of brandy, looked up. 'Before you've had a drink to help digestion?'

'I haven't the time.'

There was a call from Dolores in the kitchen. 'No doubt such unusual hurry is to meet a young woman. However, she will not make a fool of you because you will manage to do that first all by yourself.'

'I am not meeting a woman,' Alvarez replied sharply.

'Perhaps in your mind a girl half your age is not yet a woman?'

'I am going to try to help Emilio Perello, even though I ought to have enough sense not to.'

'It goes against your instincts to help anyone but yourself?'

'Since Fuster's arrested and charged him, I shouldn't go near him without Fuster's express authority.'

'Ayee! The shame of having to know that it is my own cousin who invaded Ana's sad life and turned it into bitter darkness.'

'I've said, it wasn't my fault . . .'

She swept through the bead curtain, her expression a mixture of aristocratic contempt and fishwife antagonism. 'You say Emilio is to go to the post and you will help him;

he arrives and is searched and then arrested. Had you not spoken, he would never have gone there. Even though you are a man, can you really have such shame as to say it is not your fault?'

'Because I didn't think—'

'A word of truth at last!'

'If Emilio's still being held at the post and Fuster is not there, I'll talk to Emilio and try to find a way to help.'

'Then you will do more than try, you will succeed.'

'Everything depends on what he tells me.'

'Make certain that what he says is what you need to hear.' She returned into the kitchen.

'You know what she was telling you?' Jaime muttered. 'For all our sakes, you'd better bloody well succeed.'

'I can't work miracles.'

'Then start learning how to.'

He reached across the table for the brandy.

'I thought you were in too much of a hurry?'

'Always put on a stout pair of boots before crossing a muddy field.'

'Why start talking about muddy fields? It's not rained in months.'

When Alvarez entered the post, the duty cabo looked up from the magazine he had been reading. 'You, coming in to work at this hour of the evening? Now I've seen red grass!'

'Add more water . . . Is Inspector Fuster around?'

'He was called back to Santa Amelia roughly an hour back to sort out some problem.'

'Did he say how long he expected to be away?'

'No. But if it's for his lifetime, no one here will complain.'

'Has Perello been shipped off to Palma yet?'

'Before he left, Inspector Fuster tried to arrange transport, but didn't succeed.'

'Then I'll have a word with Perello . . . There's no need to log that I've returned.'

'No one would believe me if I did.'

There were two cells, one on either side of the short passage that led from the interview room. In each heavy steel door was a spy hole and a small hatch and, below the latter, a name tag. Perello was in the cell to the left. Alvarez looked through the spy hole. On the blanket laid across the boards of the bed fixed to the floor, a thin, scraggy man lay curled up in a foetal position. A picture of despair. Alvarez returned along the corridor and crossed the interview room to the duty NCO's office.

The sargento was a large man, thanks to his wife's cooking, who was nearing retiring age. He said, his voice high with amazement: 'Is the world coming to an end?'

'Hang around and find out. I need a favour.'

'And here was I thinking it was a sense of duty brought you back . . . If you're chasing a woman and need a few thousand pesetas to make certain she doesn't run faster than you, I'm broke.'

'I need a word with Perello, but would rather Fuster didn't get to hear about this when he returns.'

'What's the idea?'

'I'm hoping to prove him wrong.'

'Then may angels escort you at the speed of light . . . The keys are where they should be which is why no one can ever find 'em.'

Alvarez lifted a large key off its labelled hook, returned to the cells, unlocked the door of the left-hand one and stepped inside.

Perello looked up, his scrawny face filled with fear, then screwed his eyes shut as if by doing so he could escape the nightmare in which he found himself.

There was a battered, stained chair against one wall and Alvarez moved this out and sat. 'I'm Enrique Alvarez. You were meant to ask for me, not Inspector Fuster, when you came here; sadly, he often get things muddled, which is why he had you locked up.'

Perello kept his eyes shut. Alvarez waited, with a peasant's indifference to passing time. Finally, Perello opened his eyes, but did not move.

'I want to help you.'

Silence.

'So when you're ready, tell me what happened.'

There was a gush of words. 'The other inspector said I killed the Englishman. I've never killed anyone. I couldn't do such a terrible thing.'

'I know that, but Inspector Fuster doesn't, so we have to make him understand.'

Another silence, then Perello slowly uncoiled. His body was in part out of proportion and the whole so ungainly that at times he seemed to be suffering some physical disability. He sat, hunched up, on the edge of the bed.

'You do understand I want to help you?' Alvarez asked.

After a moment, Perello nodded.

'So you have to tell me everything you can.'

There was another nod.

'Do you smoke?'

A third nod.

Alvarez brought a pack of cigarettes out of his pocket, offered it, helped himself. He struck a match. 'You're friends with Lucía, aren't you?'

Perello, about to light his cigarette, suddenly drew back his head. Alvarez blew out the match, dropped it on to the floor, struck another. Perello finally lit his cigarette and smoked with short, nervous puffs.

'Tell me how you met her?'

186

He took a deep breath and then spoke so quickly many of the words jumbled into each other and it became difficult to understand him. He'd been working in the hardware shop on the front. Gilberto's wife had been in charge most of the time because her husband liked to be on the beach, making friends with foreign women. She was never satisfied with the work he'd done and in the end had thrown him out because he kept forgetting to short-change the foreigners. One day – before he was thrown out – Lucía had come in to buy something the hotel needed in a hurry. She was so beautiful that . . . After she'd left, he'd dreamed about her until Gilberto's wife had shouted at him to get on with the work. That night, he'd gone to the hotel and asked if Lucía was there. She wasn't, but he'd been told where she lived. He'd begged and begged her to go out with him, but she'd said she was too busy . . . He'd asked his mother for money. He'd invited Lucía to the new restaurant which everyone was talking about and she'd finally agreed to go with him. It had cost a fortune because she had chosen the most expensive dishes.

He'd spent all the money he'd earned – that was, until he lost the job – and all the money his mother gave him, in taking Lucía to the expensive places she chose. Sometimes there had been several days when she'd said she would be too busy to see him and he'd believed her. Then she'd met the Englishman who was staying at the hotel and she'd refused to go out with him, even though she'd previously promised; when he'd begged her to change her mind, she'd told him he was only good for paying the bills when there wasn't someone better to do that. Her expressed contempt had so scrambled his mind, he'd hit her. Immediately horrified by what he'd done, he'd begged to be forgiven. She'd called him many horrible names.

Desperate, cursed by imagination and memory, he'd

asked his mother for all the money she had left and she'd given him many thousands. He'd shown them to Lucía and told her he'd take her anywhere she wanted to go. She'd called him a half-wit because he couldn't realize she'd met a real man, who could give her everything, while he could give her nothing. If he handed her a first-class round-the-world air ticket, she'd tear it up in front of him. She'd only ever gone out with him because she'd nothing better to do . . .

'You must have hated the Englishman,' Alvarez suggested casually.

'Why?'

'It was because of him that she became so cruel to you.'

Perello became lost in thought.

'Did you try to explain to the Englishman how much Lucía meant to you and how his friendship with her was hurting you?'

'I never said anything to him.'

'Why not?'

'I couldn't . . .' Perello became silent.

'Couldn't bear to meet him?'

He nodded.

The pain of facing a successful rival. 'You saw her again, didn't you, after the Englishman had left?'

He'd seen her walking along the front and, like a puppy with its tail tucked under and ears laid back, he'd sidled up and spoken to her. To his wonderment, she had not rebuffed him and soon they were back to their old relationship. And how he'd liked it, since it made him feel more wanted, when she'd told him over and over again how the swine of an Englishman had promised her a world of marvellous things and then skipped the hotel. How the other maids had jeered at her . . .

'Tell me about the cigarette lighter.'

'No,' he replied, far more forcefully than he'd spoken before.

'It's very important you do.'

'I don't know nothing.'

'It's been confirmed that it belonged to the Englishman.'

'I don't know.'

'Unless you can explain how it came to you, people like Inspector Fuster will think you stole it after you'd killed the Englishman.'

'I don't know,' he shouted.

'Did Lucía give it to you?'

'No.'

'I think she did give it to you after the body had been identified.'

He was silent.

'You must tell me if you don't want to spend years locked up in a cell even worse than this one.'

Perello suddenly flung himself backwards, then again curled up in a foetal position.

'Where does she live?'

There was no answer.

Poets wrote of the god of love whereas, if they had known the true world, they would have named the devil. Alvarez left, locked the cell door.

'Don't suppose he talked much sense?' the sargento said.

'Enough to make me interested in what he didn't say.'

'Sounds like his complaint could be catching!'

Twenty

The assistant manager at the Platjador, to whom Alvarez had spoken on his previous visit, suggested he used room 15 which would be empty until the afternoon when another busload of tourists was due to arrive. Ten minutes after he'd settled in the bedroom, Lucía entered.

'José says you want to talk to me.' Her tone was aggressive.

'I'd like a bit of a chat,' Alvarez answered easily, 'so why not sit?'

He watched her hesitate, then cross to the second chair. Perello's mother termed her puta; an exaggeration, but not a misdescription. She wore the blue cotton frock that was the 'uniform' of the hotel, but the neckline plunged deeper and the hem rode higher than on the frocks of the other maids. Her make-up was heavy, but not skilfully applied.

'Well, what is it? I've work to do and can't waste much more time in here.'

'Señorita, you'll remain until I say you may leave.'

Her expression became sullen.

'Do you know why I'm speaking to you?'

'Of course I don't.'

'It's because Emilio has been arrested.'

'Yeah? What's he done? It's got to be something bloody stupid.'

'He is accused of murdering Señor Gates.'

'He's what? You're talking daft. He hasn't the cojones to kill anybody.'

'But I'm told he beat you up?'

'All right, he knocked me about a bit and I told him just what sort of a bastard I thought that made him, but killing's different.'

'I'm glad you're as certain as I that he could not be guilty of murder.'

'What are you saying? If you've arrested him, you must think he's as guilty as hell.'

'It wasn't me and right now I'm trying to prove he's innocent. You can help me do that.'

'I don't know anything.'

'When he was searched, Emilio was found to be in possession of a lighter that belonged to Señor Gates. It is assumed by some that he stole it from the body. But if that assumption can be shown to be false, there will almost certainly not be sufficient evidence against him to hold him in jail.'

'Why tell me all that?'

'He refuses to say how he got the lighter. I'm certain you can.'

'Haven't I just said, I don't know anything?'

'Perhaps I'd better explain again. If it can be shown that Emilio gained possession of the lighter in perfect innocence, having no knowledge of where it had come from or to whom it had belonged, he will be set free.'

'So good luck to him.'

'Have you any idea of what it's like for a person of his nature to be banged up in a tiny cell?'

'How could I?'

'By using your imagination and realizing that he's scared to the centre of his backbone. You owe him your help.'

'I don't owe him anything.'

'It's amused you to let him entertain you when there's been no one else willing to spend more on you than he does. Amusement costs.'

'I ain't going to be insulted like this.'

'There are more insults to come. You are a thief.'

'I ain't never pinched anything.'

'Señor Gates has always chased the pleasures of life and so when he saw you – was it cleaning the bathroom? – he made an old-fashioned play and led you to believe he was very wealthy and would share that wealth with you in return for your sharing his bed.'

'That's a bleeding lie.'

'But when it became clear to you that he saw the relationship as no more than a one-night stand, you had to accept he'd been using you as you'd been using Emilio and that hurt. But there didn't seem to be any way of getting your own back until you saw his lighter lying around the bedroom. Guessing how much it meant to him, you took it—'

'I never ever even saw it.'

'You kept it as a memento to ease your battered pride until you learned Señor Gates had been murdered. That frightened you and you realized you'd better get rid of it. But as it was obviously worth a bit, you couldn't bring yourself to throw it away and decided to give it to Emilio because then you'd be able to have many a silent laugh, seeing the man you mocked using the lighter which had belonged to the man who'd mocked you.'

'You bastard!' she said violently.

'And to make certain your theft would never come to light, you made Emilio promise he'd never tell anyone how he'd got it. You knew he'd hold to that promise even to his own cost.'

'You're crazy.'

192

'Just making you understand you have to help free an innocent man.'

'I don't know anything.'

He experienced a sharp uneasiness. What he was about to suggest would be a lie and justice was truth; yet a truly honest man would admit there were times when lies helped justice, while truth damned it. 'You don't need to admit you stole the lighter.'

'I'll tell you again. I never even saw the bloody thing.'

'If you claim Señor Gates gave it to you as a token of thanks, I won't dispute that.'

'You think I'm going to stick out my head so as you can kick it?'

'Say what I've suggested and Emilio will be released.'

'And I'm supposed to risk everything and rush to get him back when he's just a nuisance, always hanging around like a starving dog?'

Alvarez stood. 'You leave me with no choice but to prove you stole the lighter.'

'And that's supposed to have me shivering?' she sneered. 'From the look of you, you'd have trouble proving you're alive.'

He left the room and returned in the lift to the ground floor. He met the assistant manager in the middle of the foyer. 'Everything satisfactory?' the other asked cheerfully.

As Alvarez drew level with the desk, the duty cabo said: 'Your lovely mate's been shouting for you ever since he arrived back here and found you weren't killing yourself with work.'

'I've been down in the port, questioning a possible witness.'

'And Julia Roberts has promised to go to Monte Carlo with me.'

'Only because she's never had the misfortune to meet you.'

He carried on up to the room that was now his, slumped down in the chair. On his return home the previous evening, Dolores had belligerently demanded to know if she could ring Antonia and tell her she could assure Ana that there was no need for any more heart-aching worry? 'Not just yet, but soon,' he'd answered. 'It is to be hoped for many people's sake that it is very soon.' She might as well have been expecting him to dig up the pot of gold at the end of the rainbow. As things stood, the only way of ensuring Emilio's release was to identify the murderer . . . What if Lucía was telling the truth? After all, the quality of her character didn't inescapably brand her a liar in all matters and it was only his own assumption, based on little more than a sequence of events and times that fitted that assumption, which named her thief. If she really never had seen that lighter and had not stolen it in a gesture of anger, then Emilio was the thief and that made him prime suspect. But if he had the cunning the murderer had shown, could she have pulled the wool over his eyes as tightly as she had? Was love ever quite that blind?

If not Emilio, who? Motive and character had to be the essentials. Which brought Gomilio back into view. And it occurred to Alvarez that he had not, as perhaps he should have done, ascertained the colour and make of Gomilio's car and checked (hadn't Fuster wanted him to do this?) whether it had been seen at the relevant time near the point where Gates's body had been found. Yet unless Gomilio's car was unusual in some respect, who would have noticed it so carefully as to remember it almost a month later? The chances of success were so small they became insignificant when one considered the effort that would be required to pursue the line of inquiry . . .

The door swung back and startled him. Fuster stepped inside. He raised his left wrist and ostentatiously looked at his watch. 'You keep ever more unusual working hours.'

'I've been down in the port, questioning Lucía Ortega.'

'Why?'

'To try to make her admit she gave Gates's lighter to Perello.'

'Did you succeed?'

'No.'

'Hardly surprising since it is clear he stole it after murdering Gates . . . Because I believe a working relationship calls for openness in some matters, you should know that earlier this morning I spoke to the superior chief and made a complaint concerning you.'

'A "working relationship" gains a whole new meaning. What is my latest crime? Have I filed a report in the wrong place?'

'To the best of my knowledge, you have not filed a single report since I have been in command here . . . Yesterday evening, you returned and questioned Perello, knowing this was forbidden unless with my authority.'

'Who says I did that?'

'When I told Perello he was to be taken to Palma prison, he became hysterical and repeatedly said that last night you had promised to save him.'

'It is a sad fact that the dog most likely to bite you is the one you're trying to free from a trap.'

'A nonsensical statement.'

'Because you would always leave it in the trap? . . . What was the superior chief's response to the news?'

'Naturally, to me, it was neutral.'

'Then he can't have been feeling up to scratch.'

'I have no doubt he will speak to you about the matter when the time is convenient.'

'A pleasure in store.'

'Since the case is now solved, I shall be leaving before lunch and returning to Santa Amelia.'

'Another pleasure to look forward to.'

Fuster left.

Alvarez settled back in the chair. Soon, very soon, he would be returning to his room – space, comfort, a desk with a bottom right-hand drawer. The future would have been all sunshine had it not been for the fact that if Emilio was innocent, as he believed, every effort was going to have to be made to free him.

Twenty-One

Returning late in the afternoon, Alvarez entered his own room to find to his consternation that Fuster sat behind the desk. 'You told me you were leaving before lunch.'

'That certainly was my intention. However, the superior chief rang and since then I have decided to begin a more concentrated effort to bring order to this office. A task I have no hesitation in calling the thirteenth labour.'

'What did he say to change your mind?'

'I have always maintained that properly filed records are the backbone of police work, yet I have not found anything in this desk or the cabinet in chronological order and properly indexed.'

'Everything that looks as if it could be important goes into one of the desk drawers and what's on top came in latest. Why was Salas ringing?'

'Initially, he expressed his surprise at learning you had already left the post when he rang. Had he rung again after lunch, I don't doubt his surprise at your continuing absence would have been even greater.'

'It was me he wanted?'

'Indeed.'

'Why?'

'Following his expressions of surprise, he remarked that undoubtedly if asked to explain your early departure, you'd reply you went down to the port to question a prospective witness. With the dry wit which so characterizes him, he observed that Port Llueso contains so many prospective witnesses, there can be little room for honest tourists. Now, I'll thank you to leave me to try to bring order out of chaos.'

'You still haven't said what the superior chief wanted.'

'As to that, no doubt he will be speaking to you in the near future.'

Alvarez went down the corridor to the shoebox of a room he thought he'd finally quit and slumped down in the chair. The earlier clouds on the horizon had thickened and rolled forward to cover the sky. At lunch, Dolores had observed long silences; could other women use silence as a lethal threat of troubled times to come? Fuster was still in 'his room' and now seemed to expect to remain there for some time yet. Salas was going to ring again. Troubles were never lonely.

Twenty minutes later, the telephone rang and jerked him fully awake.

'No doubt you learned little from the prospective witness?' was Salas's greeting.

Very droll! 'Señor, I decided I should make a wide-ranging assessment of the area in the mountains where Señor Gates's body was found in order to decide whether the time and effort involved in trying to find a witness who saw his hire car within the relevant times would be justified. Basically, there are so few homes and so little land which can be cultivated that not many local people are ever around. There is some traffic on the road because tourists drive or are driven to Laraix Monastery, but almost all of those who were on the island then will have returned to their home countries by now; perhaps a driver of one of the tourist buses would remember the car because of some particular feature, but the odds against that have to be very great. So can the effort be justified?'

'And the answer is?'

'It's virtually impossible to give one. The odds against winning the lottery are perhaps even greater, but normally each draw is won by someone.'

'Hardly a relevant comparison. What is the purpose of tracing a person who saw the car?'

'To find out if he, or she, can identify who was driving it.'

'You do not find that obvious? If before his death, Gates was; if after, Perello.'

'I don't believe Perello was ever within many kilometres of the car. Again if Gomilio's . . .'

'Does that explain why you ignored the rules of procedure and questioned him without Inspector Fuster's approval after he'd been arrested and charged?'

'I've always held, señor, that there can be a time when a rule needs to be broken.'

'Surely what you hold is the proposition that there is none which should be kept?'

'Where innocence is at stake, perhaps that is so.'

'You see yourself as being entitled to judge innocence and guilt?'

'I'm certain Perello is innocent of Señor Gates's death.'

'Inspector Fuster disagrees with you. I have the greatest confidence in his handling of this case.'

'He's convinced Perello stole the lighter from the body. I believe it was given to him some time after Gates died.'

'Given by whom?'

'Lucía Ortega.'

'Who is she?'

'Perello would probably describe her as his novia. She would contemptuously deny that and it's surely proof of Perello's lack of intelligence, street cred, knowledge of women, that's he's never really realized the true nature of their relationship.'

'Which is what?'

'He's the fall-back so when there's no one better around,
to keep him happy, she feeds him every now and then.'

'What do feeding habits have to do with this case?'

'I wasn't referring to food, señor.'

'Then what?'

'In certain circumstances, what a man expects after he's
taken a woman to an expensive restaurant.'

'Dammit, Alvarez, first you're talking about food, then
you're not, then you are. Have you the slightest idea what
you're saying?'

'Señor, a man may expect to be paid.'

'Only if he is a gigolo.'

'I wasn't talking about money.'

'A man expects to be paid, but you're not talking about
money! To speak nonsense once may be viewed as an
innocent aberration; to do so twice smacks of insolence.'

There were none so blind as refused to understand. 'Señor,
by payment, I meant sex.'

There was a silence.

'Experience,' Salas finally said, 'should have warned me
that even in a conversation concerning a cigarette lighter,
you would introduce the subject.'

'Sex is important . . .'

'An opinion that, had you even a modicum of self-respect,
you would not hold, let alone broadcast.'

'But it is important in this case. I'm certain Perello
promised he'd never say where the lighter came from and
so refuses to do so, even though an ounce of common
sense would make him realize he must. He's been blinded
by sex—'

'I have heard more than enough. Had I had doubts about
the future course to take, they would now be set firmly to
rest. A man who delights in wallowing in lasciviousness is

not fit to be in a position of authority. Therefore, subject to any condition the director general may be pleased to make, the Llueso and Santa Amelia areas will be amalgamated, with Inspector Fuster in charge, thereby ensuring not only a high degree of efficiency, but also a proper regard for the proprieties.'

'You . . . you're saying I'm going to have to continue to work under him?'

'I am.'

'Señor, you can't do that.'

'As is normal, you are mistaken. I have only one more point to make. Should a false sense of pride make you reluctant to accept the change, you can be assured your resignation will be accepted without argument.' Salas cut the connexion.

Alvarez slowly replaced the receiver. Because of the course their conversation had taken, he had not received a verbal lashing for breaking the rules by questioning Perello, but of what comfort was that when faced with the prospect of Fuster's continuing in command? Time would be sanctified, every rule would have to be strictly observed; meriendas in Club Llueso would have to be hurried, perhaps even abandoned; siestas would be cut so short they would be mere shadows . . .

One could not change the past or set the future, but one could sometimes ease the pain of the present. He left the room, made his way downstairs and out into the road. He was halfway across the old square and heading directly for the Club Llueso when a woman's voice behind him said: 'Hullo, Inspector.'

He turned to face Iris Perry. 'Good evening, señorita.' She was looking very attractive, he thought; only one or two lines in her face, highlighted by the sunshine, betrayed the fact that she was older than first impressions might suggest.

201

It was almost akin to magic, the way in which women could sometimes visually shed a few years.

'I do hope—' she began, then stopped as she was pushed aside by a beer-bellied tourist. Once the twenty-five-year-old was past, quite unaware that his manners matched his appearance, she said: 'I do hope nothing's wrong. You look rather as if – as my father used to say – the tax demand has arrived by the same post as the overdraft figures.' She suddenly waved and called out: 'Over here, Basil.'

Perry eased his way through the swirl of tourists. 'Can't leave you on your own for five minutes or you find yourself a man! . . . Nice to meet again, Inspector. How's life?'

'It has its ups and downs, señor.'

'And right now, more downs than ups,' she said. 'But there I go for the second time, making personal remarks.'

'Your forte, my sweet.' Perry smiled.

'They're not meant meanly.'

'Who could imagine such a possibility?'

'You obviously could, from your tone.'

He laughed. 'A typical uncharitable wifely observation . . . But why are we standing in the full sun, surrounded by the world and his wives, when we should be sitting and sipping? You'll join us, Inspector?'

'That would be a pleasure, señor.'

They climbed the steps and crossed to a table that enjoyed the shade of one of the trees. A waiter, perspiring freely, took their order.

Perry brought a cigarette case from his pocket. 'I don't remember – do you smoke?'

'I'm afraid so.'

'Isn't it ridiculous how authority has made us ashamed of everything that gives pleasure?' He opened the case, held it out. 'What motivates their desire to equate enjoyment with sin? Is it the realization that if we all learned to enjoy pleasure unreservedly, authority would become redundant?'

'Smoking is bad for your health and I wish you'd give it up,' Iris said.

'You also would deny me pleasure?'

'If it denies you an early grave, yes.'

'Then I haven't yet become the traditional elderly husband, an encumbrance?'

'I wish you wouldn't talk like that.'

'For fear the inspector thinks my puerile humour has an edge to it because our marriage isn't all light and sweetness? I'm sure he has judged better than that and knows it's still flourishing.' He turned. 'Am I not right?'

'Indeed, señor,' Alvarez replied, not quite certain to what he was assenting.

'He had to say that from politeness.'

'If I read the Mallorquin character correctly, they don't follow our example and turn politeness into hypocrisy.'

The waiter returned, put the glasses on the table, spiked the bill, hurried away.

Perry raised his glass. 'What do we drink to? How about the present? Enjoying drinks as we are, where we are, is as near perfection as we mortals are normally permitted to enjoy.'

'I'm pretty certain the present isn't all that good for the inspector.'

Perry turned to Alvarez. 'I hope I haven't clumsily caused offence?'

'Señor, it brings pleasure to see someone so content and happy.'

'But things aren't like that for you?'

'The future is at fault, not the present . . . There is to be a reorganization in the Cuerpo.'

'And that will adversely affect you?'

'I will lose my independent command and have to serve directly under another officer. Unfortunately, he and I look at almost everything from different viewpoints.'

'Is it becoming rudely inquisitive to ask in what way?'

'For him, there is always a straight line; for me, there is sometimes a curve.'

'How right you are! Dear old Euclid got it wrong when he claimed the shortest distance between A and B was never via C. Ask any politician. They use curves to such an extent that sometimes they stab themselves in their backs . . . In time, your colleague will probably realize you're right.'

'I doubt that. He is so certain he always knows best that it will be me who will have to change.'

'Then you had cause to look so worried. To change one's friends can be an advantage, to change oneself is always a disadvantage.'

'Sub-Oscar,' she said.

'No marks for effort? . . . Inspector, you will, won't you, have the other half as a prophylactic against the future?' He signalled to a waiter, who came across and took the order.

Conscious that his own problems were hardly a welcome topic of discussion, Alvarez changed the conversation. 'I hope the sailing has been good?'

'It's been too lazy,' she answered.

Perry laughed. 'You reckon true sailing never starts under a force six wind. I'm far more restful. For me, there are times when light airs are fine. The painted ship upon the painted ocean.'

'You talk like that now, yet you're the restless one.'

'Surely a different kind of restlessness?'

She spoke to Alvarez. 'I'd choose to stay here. Our lease

ends in a few days and we can renew it. But Basil's suffering ever more itchy feet and wants to sail on and see more of the Mediterranean before winter closes things down.'

'Somewhere out there,' Perry said, 'there's that little Greek island which is even closer to paradise than here.'

'In your mind, maybe, but in fact? If it's undiscovered by tourism, it's probably too primitive for your sophisticated tastes; if discovered, it'll be swamped with hotels, discos, and lager louts. But here, they've somehow managed to keep a reasonable balance between tourists and a pleasant life.'

The waiter returned and put down three glasses, picked up the empty ones, left.

Perry raised his glass. 'Here's hoping my little Greek island doesn't turn into a fata morgana and earn me a heartfelt, "Told you so."'

She reached across and put her right hand on his left arm. 'I promise I won't say that.'

'Or think it?'

'I'll try very hard not to. And the wonderful things is, we can always return here and put down our roots.'

The way she looked at her husband brought Alvarez sudden, sharp, brief mental pain; Juana María had often looked at him with such an expression and even after all the intervening years, he could still remember how a heavenly choir had struck up whenever she did . . .

Love could soothe even those who weren't involved and merely observed. When, fifteen minutes later, he made his way back to the post, the world was a happier place. It was unfortunate that almost as soon as he sat, Fuster hurried into the room.

'Where have you been? Searching for prospective witnesses?'

Made careless by the other's aggressive attitude, Alvarez

replied: 'Having a couple of drinks in the square with some English friends.'

'Is that supposed to be humorous?'

'Only to someone with a sense of humour.'

Despite the heat, Fuster was wearing a linen jacket and tie; he fiddled with the knot of the tie. 'Have you spoken to the superior chief?'

'More times than I care to remember.'

'I am referring to today.'

'He rang earlier.'

'He has told you he proposes to amalgamate the two areas and I shall be in command?'

'Yes.'

'Then it will help if you understand from the beginning that there will be a number of changes, designed to bring about the same high degree of efficiency with which I ran my previous area. All incoming reports, memoranda, and notices will be indexed and filed on receipt; not in chaos in drawers, but on the computer . . .'

'What computer?'

'I am indenting for one. It will be up to you to learn as soon as possible how to operate this.'

'I can't cope with something like that.'

'Every crime report will first be referred to me, where-upon I will decide how the investigation is to proceed – at the same time, naturally, your crime diary will be kept up to date. Phone calls will be logged and, when necessary, cross-indexed to what action results from them. Normal working hours will be observed and noted.'

'What's that mean?'

'Every arrival and departure from the post will be written down and, where applicable, the reason for leaving the post.'

'If I'm going to have my hair cut, I have to note that down?'

'Members of the Cuerpo do not have their hair cut during working hours. The fact you need to be reminded of this goes a long way to explaining why the number of arrests in the area – when recorded – are the lowest on the island.'

'That's because fewer crimes are committed. Why? Because I don't waste my time filing, I don't bother to note down everything I do, I go out and about, talk and listen.'

'In the bar at Club Llueso?'

'It wouldn't occur to you that one of the most productive places for gathering information is a bar?'

'Drunken information, as worthless as a plumber's promise . . . As from tomorrow morning, you will report here by eight and I will then detail your work for the day.'

'At eight tomorrow morning, I'm starting to try to find someone who saw Gates's and/or Angel Gomilio's car on the road near where the body was found.'

'With what object?'

'Proving Perello did not murder Gates.'

'You will not waste time on so pointless a task. As I have just said, you will report here—'

'Until the director general agrees to the amalgamation, this remains my area and I give the orders. Tomorrow morning, I'll be up in the mountains.'

Fuster hesitated, then turned and left, slamming the door shut behind himself.

Alvarez stared at the far wall. Sometimes a battle won was a war lost. He had the uncomfortable feeling that this was one such occasion.

Twenty-Two

W hen Alvarez returned home on Saturday evening, supper was almost finished. Dolores put down the banana she had been about to peel. 'We waited for as long as we could, but the children were in a hurry to go off.'

He spoke wearily. 'I was told about a man who might be able to help and it took me twice as long as I expected to find him. He knew nothing.'

'You've been up in the mountains all this time?'

He nodded.

'Your meal's keeping warm in the oven and I'll get it for you. Unless you'd like a drink before you eat?'

Did he admit that or, for the possible sake of peace, deny it? 'I won't have one if it'll upset things.'

'Another few minutes won't do your meal any harm. And you look worn out. It'll do you good.'

Jaime said reproachfully: 'You never tell me a drink will do me good.'

'When did you last work all day and come home tired? When did you last work? I ask you to mend the kitchen shutters and what happens? You sit in front of the television.'

'I said, I'll do that just as soon as I've had a word with Benito to find out the best way of making the repair.'

'And you are most likely to have that word sitting in front of the television?' She saw Alvarez settle. 'Pass Enrique the coñac.'

'He's that tired he can't reach for it?' Jaime unscrewed the cap of the bottle.

'There's no call for you to have any more.'

'I was only saving him trouble. I'll swear that if I saw a woman drowning and swam out to save her, you'd say—'

'That she must be young and attractive, or you'd not have bothered. Is there any ice left?'

Alvarez looked into the insulated container. 'It's melted, so I'll get some more.'

'Stay where you are.' She reached across and picked up the container, went through to the kitchen.

'What makes her treat you like you're suddenly covered in honey?' Jaime asked resentfully.

'Because she knows I've been a busy bee,' Alvarez answered.

'If I'd wanted some ice, you know what she'd have said?'

'That you could enjoy your first exercise of the day and get it,' she called out from the kitchen, just before she returned and handed the container to Alvarez. He picked out three ice cubes and dropped them into the brandy he had already poured. He drank. A pleasure delayed was a pleasure augmented.

She peeled her banana. 'It's three days now you've been going up into the mountains.'

He nodded.

'Looking more and more tired when you return.'

'In this heat, it's hard work visiting the houses and if the man isn't around – and when is he? – tramping the land until I find him.'

'You've not learned anything?'

'Nothing. Vehicles in Palma tell me Gomilio owns a red Astra. So I ask people, did you see a red Astra parked by the side of the road near the oak tree that was struck by lightning.

The person to whom I'm speaking looks at me as if I am mad. Who remembers something of no concern that happened a month ago? When one has to make a living from poor land, who has time to waste looking at parked cars? The drivers of the coaches laugh. Do I think they have nothing better to do, with their buses filled with ill-behaved foreigners, than to make a mental note of every car they pass?'

'So what can you do now?'

He drained the glass, refilled it, watched with angry jealousy by Jaime. As he added ice, he said: 'Keep searching. I've spoken to maybe forty people. Perhaps the forty-first will be able to tell me something useful.'

'You still think you will find someone who can?'

He drank. 'The odds are increasingly against that. I have spoken to virtually everyone who lives or works near the road. Now I have to move further into the mountains since there are still some willing to live in such isolation.'

'You are doing too much.'

'At least by the end I will know I could have done nothing more.'

'If you come back night after night, so tired you are like a sleepwalker—'

Jaime interrupted her. 'Do sleepwalkers drink like he's drinking?'

'Ayee! How a woman suffers who is married to a man who cannot understand it is better to remain silent than to speak mindless stupidities.' She turned back to Alvarez. 'I will tell Ana that everything which could be done to help her Emilio has been.'

'Not yet,' Alvarez said. 'Leave that until I'm absolutely certain I can't find anyone who saw Gomilio's car.'

'You have just told me it is almost impossible you will.'

'Yet somewhere there may be someone who was on the road at the right time and noticed the red Astra and for a

210

reason, remembers it. Whilst that possibility exists, I have to keep going.'

'Not if you do too much and ruin your health.'

'I won't do that.'

'You think that at your age you can ignore your body?'

'You always say men never think of anything else—' Jaime began.

'Be quiet,' she hissed. 'Enrique, I feel very sad for Ana, which is why I asked you to help her. But you must not go on and on at your own expense. If nothing more can reasonably be done by you, Ana must pray that somehow, someone else will make the future brighter for her.'

He put his glass down on the table. 'I'm going to continue. But that's not for Ana's sake, not even for Emilio's.'

'Then why?'

'I am convinced Emilio is innocent so it is for innocence's sake I will go on. I have tried to convince Fuster that that is what justice means, but he is a man who considers only rules, who ignores emotion and instinct, who will always try not to do something that might prove him wrong. So there is only me to continue to try and prove innocence.'

She pushed her chair back, stood, moved to put her hand on Alvarez's shoulder. 'You're a good man, Enrique. Now I will get your meal.' She left.

Jaime said: 'Where's the sense in saying you're not going to work for Emilio's sake when that's just what you're going to be doing?'

'The concept of justice is more important than an individual's injustice.'

'Is that supposed to make sense?'

'It does to me.'

Jaime was silent for a moment. When he next spoke, he lowered his voice until one or two of his words were not

very clear. 'And what's got her saying you're a good man?
It's not like her to talk soft.'

'Maybe she's taking a kinder view of life.'

'Then . . .' Jaime looked at the bead curtain, hastily
reached across for the bottle of brandy and poured himself
a drink.

On Monday, sweating and short of breath, Alvarez climbed
the stairs and began to walk along the corridor. As he passed
the open doorway of 'his room', there was a call; he stopped,
stepped inside.

'It's a quarter past eight,' Fuster said.

'Twelve minutes past by my watch.'

'I think I made the point that from now on, good time-
keeping will be a feature of my command?'

'I had trouble starting my car.'

'If you walked to work, you would avoid such a possibility; in addition, you would enjoy a little of the exercise
you so obviously need.'

'Do the rules of procedure say I have to walk to work?'

'Of course not.'

'Then I'll continue to drive.'

Fuster's thin lips tightened. 'In view of certain facts,
I have spoken to the superior chief and asked whether
you are justified in claiming that until the director general agrees to the amalgamation, you remain in overall
charge of this area while I am in command of the particular case. His reply was unequivocal. Such agreement is
solely an administrative matter and in practical terms, his
decision is final. Consequently, I am now, and have been,
in overall tactical and strategic command of both areas. Is
that clear?'

'Yes.'

'You insisted you were going to search for someone who

had noted Gates's or Gomilio's car on the Friday. Is that what you've been doing?'

'Yes.'

'Have you found an eyewitness?'

'No.'

'Hardly surprising. Common sense said that that was impossible. However, you suffer the islanders' inability to recognize common sense . . . Let me make something sufficiently clear that you will be unable to misunderstand it. From this moment, you will waste no more time on a fruitless search.'

Alvarez went to speak, checked the words. Then he said: 'We don't like each other, but we have to work together, so can't we call a truce?'

'What are you trying to say?'

'That if there's the faintest possibility Gomilio is guilty and his car was in the mountains that day . . .'

'There is none. Perello has been charged with the murder and the investigation is completed.'

'You cannot imagine you might be wrong?'

'I work to fact, not groundless supposition.'

'Just give me a couple more days up in the mountains. Then, if I still have drawn a blank . . .'

'You will work to my orders.'

'The thought you may have arrested an innocent man doesn't worry you?'

'I have control of my imagination.'

Alvarez left. In the room he was now occupying, he slumped down on the chair. Because he was forbidden to return to the mountains, he suffered the certainty that somewhere amongst the swathes of pine trees, holm oaks, and thick undergrowth, the steep foothills and the occasional terraced land, there was someone who had noted the car, or something lying on the ground, who or which could confirm

Perello's innocence. But he would never know unless he continued the search. Yet so open a refusal to obey orders must lead to his dismissal from the force . . . On one side of the scales, a man's innocence; on the other, his own career. He cursed himself for a coward as he recognized that career weighed more heavily.

Twenty-Three

Throughout July, the temperature rose and then August brought new heat records. Day after day, it remained above 35 and on one weekend reached 41. Chemists had difficulty in keeping stocked with sunburn lotions, doctors tut-tutted over badly burned bodies as they wondered what new cars to buy, local ice cream manufacturers worked throughout the nights, waiters became exhausted and bars had to be closed before the owners wished; in the fields, animals sought whatever shade there was and stood motionless for hour after hour, waiting for the lesser heat of the night before they tried to find something to eat; shallow wells had long since dried up and even deep ones were providing only a proportion of the water they normally did, while those near the coast were becoming more contaminated with salt water.

Alvarez mopped his face and neck for the umpteenth time and cursed the heat for the umpteenth time; icebergs and metre-deep snowfalls haunted the corners of his mind . . .

The phone rang and the plum-voiced secretary said the superior chief wished to speak to him. He waited, receiver to ear; this was the first call from Salas for a long while – there was one very small benefit from Fuster's having taken full command . . .

'Good morning,' Salas said.

Alvarez stared with astonishment at the opened, but not

yet shuttered, window. The superior chief condescending to
wish him a good morning . . .

'Are you there?'

Hurriedly, he replied: 'Yes, señor.'

'How are you finding things?'

'What things exactly?' he asked uneasily, wondering what
thunderbolt was about to be launched.

'Working with Inspector Fuster. I expect you're getting
on well with him?'

Which showed how wrong a superior chief's expectations
could be. 'Yes, señor.'

'Good.'

There was a long pause.

Salas coughed. 'I'm sure you will appreciate that the
proposed amalgamation is in the name of efficiency and in
no way an adverse reflection on yourself? You must know
that Inspector Fuster has expressed his considerable regard
for your talents.'

Things had become absurd. The superior chief was mad,
drunk, or stoned.

'Which is why I have decided . . . Perhaps I should start at
the beginning. Always a good idea, don't you think?' There
was a sound that could have been a laugh.

Salas was obviously drunk.

'Earlier today, I received a telephone call from District
Attorney Setsalnikos, whose authority covers the island of
Siphogos, which is, I understand, in the Dodecanese group.
Do you happen to know it?'

'No, señor.'

'Very beautiful, he told me, though somewhat under-
developed. He seemed apologetic on that score, but there are
many who would claim that as a prime virtue, aren't there?'

'Yes, señor.' When the impossible happened, sense
became nonsense, nonsense, sense.

'I spoke to him through an interpreter, modern Greek not being one of my languages. Do you speak it?'

'No, señor.'

'I doubt anyone not obliged to do so does. However, that is besides the point. District Attorney Setsalnikos – it would help if they had more easily pronounceable names – informed me that under existing law there cannot be an arrest without the issue of a warrant when more than twenty-four hours have elapsed since the incident in question. As he said quite frankly, his problem is, does he, or doesn't he, issue a warrant; the presence of a foreigner inevitably makes a law officer's task more difficult. He asked if we could help him and naturally I assured him we would do everything in our power. Willing assistance given with no ulterior motive is good for public relations, isn't it?'

'Yes, señor.'

'As he remarked, the basic problem is the difficulty in distinguishing between an accident and murder camouflaged as an accident, but the fierce row between them has to be very relevant in making that distinction. I'm sure you'd agree with that?'

'Probably, señor, but I'm afraid I can't quite follow what's happened.'

'If you'd listen—' Salas began angrily, then abruptly stopped. When he next spoke, his tone was as pleasant, and falsely so, as it had been before. 'Perhaps I have not explained things as clearly as I might wish. Indeed . . . Well, I have to confess the course of events unusually leaves me very undecided. Do you ever find you can place two opposing conclusions on the same set of facts?'

'Yes, señor.'

'Very perplexing . . . I did ask questions to try to gain a more definitive viewpoint, but unfortunately he clearly has difficulty on concentrating on what is pertinent. He insisted

217

on telling me about a foreign woman who owns part of the island and leads a life of debauchery. I naturally thought she must have played some large part in the case, but it seemed that it was only a very minor one. There really was no need for him to discuss her as he did. It is extraordinary how there are people who revel in lascivious details, isn't it?'

'Yes, señor.'

'Most regrettable. Perhaps all Greeks have an unhealthy interest in such matters. Indeed, more than once I have read references to the Greek way of love.'

Alvarez wondered with dismay if he were going to be called upon to explain what that might be.

'Although barely touched by normal tourism, Siphogos apparently is something of a mecca for yachtsmen and during the summer there are always a number of yachts anchored along the coast – there is no marina. Last Sunday night, people on one yacht heard the couple – whom they'd briefly met – on another yacht having a very bitter row. The Tomkins naturally assumed it was a case of too much drink since the parties concerned were English.

'The next morning – the Monday – the Tomkins watched the other yacht sail off and they waved to the couple aboard, who waved back; in so far as they could judge, peace had been restored. That afternoon, the other yacht returned with the wife in hysterics and her husband unconscious, having suffered a very severe blow to his head. A doctor was called from the neighbouring island, but by the time he arrived, the husband was dead. Naturally, the police were summoned. When asked what had happened, the wife stated that while at sea, she'd been in the cabin, preparing a meal, when there'd been a very fierce wind squall which had taken them . . . Is aback the right word?'

'I'm afraid I'm no yachtsman.'

'The boom swung across very suddenly and violently and caught her husband on the side of his head. Apparently, a tragic accident. But Setsalnikos, who spent a long time telling me what a good yachtsman he is, says that for the husband to have been struck as described, he must have been standing tall – whatever that means – and to have utterly failed to notice the approaching wind squall even though this is a recognized hazard, mentioned in all sailing directions, near the island due to some meteorological peculiarity. In other words, the husband acted as if he were a tyro. But the Tomkins state that when earlier talking to the other couple, it became clear from what the husband said that he had been sailing for very many years and, in fact, was something of an expert.

'Setsalnikos put this contradiction to the wife and she insisted very wildly that her husband was indeed a very accomplished yachtsman. Clearly, this raises the possibility of murder presented as an accident and the row on the previous night could be of the greatest consequence. It is to try to resolve the problem of whether it was accident or murder that Setsalnikos is asking for our assistance. Is everything now clear?'

'I don't understand why he thinks we could help him.'

'The wife has repeatedly claimed we would confirm she could not have murdered her husband because we know she loved him – as she put it very theatrically – to the centre of her heart.'

'But we can't know anything of the sort.'

'Nevertheless, having assured the district attorney we will do all we can, I'm sure you'll help to the best of your considerable ability.'

'Why me?'

'Because the wife has named you.'

'Then who on earth is she?'

There was a long silence. Finally, Salas said: 'Señora Perry.'

Alvarez expressed his surprise in earthy Mallorquin, than which there is no earthier.

'There is no need for such language,' Salas said weakly, not understanding what had been said, but convinced he would have been very offended if he had.

'If it was an accident, it's not our concern, if murder, there has to be a connexion with Gates's murder,' Alvarez said.

'To accept that is to hold the Perrys were actually a party to the murder and you have repeatedly assured me they can't have been because they had absolutely no motive.'

'They didn't.'

'Then how can the possibility of Señora Perry's involvement in her husband's murder be in any way connected?'

'If there isn't a connecting link, the coincidence is extraordinary.'

'Coincidences happen.'

'Nevertheless, I'm sure this isn't one.'

'What's your reason for saying that?'

'At the moment, just instinct,' Alvarez replied rashly. To his surprise, his comment was met with silence, not a sarcastic reprimand for confusing mumbo-jumbo with criminal detection. The silence told him more than a hundred words. It explained Salas's pleasant attitude; it said that, against his will, Salas accepted the two deaths probably were linked; that if this were so, then Perello was innocent . . .

It was a moment to savour; a moment to forget that one did not kick a man when he was down. 'It seems very likely Inspector Fuster acted injudiciously when he insisted on arresting Perello.'

'I really don't think one should say that on the grounds of what is no more than an assumption.'

'An assumption which has to be checked. How do we do

that?' Made rash by the sense of triumph, he spoke to Salas as if to an equal.

'Talk to Setsalnikos over the phone and find out exactly what Señora Perry—'

'I think I should go there and question her.'

'I don't see the need for that.'

'No need, when Perello is in prison and I have many, many times stated my belief in his innocence on the grounds of the evidence, but Inspector Fuster has always chosen not to listen to me? If Señora Perry's evidence can prove Perello's innocence, we must ascertain what that evidence is at the first possible moment. How would things look if we don't? Innocence held in jail despite the objections of one of the inspectors engaged in the investigation, innocence held in jail far longer than necessary because an inspector was prevented from travelling to Greece . . . Anti-authority media would tear the Cuerpo's reputation to shreds.'

'Very well,' Salas muttered, before he replaced the receiver.

Alvarez settled back in the chair. Several days away from the office; the chance to prove Fuster wrong; the possibility of proving Perello's innocence and so to free him . . . Not even the thought of having to fly could dim his sense of wonderment at the twists and turns of life.

Approached from the north-west, Siphogos was first a dark, irregularly shaped mountain that stuck out of the wine-dark sea like an emergent volcano; nearer, the one mountain became many, closely grouped together and framed by the blue sky, a small, white cloud streaming from the highest peak; close to, stone houses, stone walls, and a road that clung to the side of the most westerly mountain; once tied up to the rickety-looking jetty, oak, fir, pine, walnut, cherry, citrus, and olive trees, vegetables, and small, irregularly shaped fields of stubble were visible.

Alvarez was keen to leave the ferry – from the moment of boarding, he'd doubted so ancient a craft could survive a rough sea – but to do so meant walking down the gangway. He waited and waited, then, showing a courage only he could ever appreciate, stepped off the ferry and, struggling to think of anything but the space beneath him, gripping the rope on either side, he made his way down to the wooden planking of the jetty. Altophobia could make the strong weak; it turned him into a quivering wreck.

A small, thin man, with a strongly featured and darkly complexioned face, came up.

He said in Spanish, speaking with such difficulty that it was obvious he had learned the few words only with the greatest difficulty: 'You the Inspector Alvarez? . . . Welcome.' They shook hands.

'Do you speak English?' Alvarez asked.

Tzoumakas did and communication became much easier. He suggested they went first to the Hotel Zeria – which, he hoped their guest would understand, was not luxurious, no hotel on the island was, but was clean – and afterwards they could have a drink whilst they discussed matters. Later, they could drive the short distance to Edissovas, the second largest village on the island, where Iris Perry was staying. Her yacht was tied up and the accommodation had been secured so there was no fear of her trying to sail away; the crew of the ferry had been told to make certain she did not board unless police permission had been given for her to leave Siphogos.

As they drove along the road which lay between the beach of sand and several small fields under cultivation, Alvarez wondered if there would be more than retsina to drink. Benito, who'd spent time in Greece, had told him that not

even the lees served to tourists in Mallorca when they were
drunk tasted quite so awful.

'It is beautiful, no?' Tzoumakas waved his right hand.

'Very attractive,' Alvarez agreed politely. Several yachts
were anchored close in-shore, their mastheads tracing only
the smallest of patterns against the sky; the sand was golden,
the sea was clear and shoals of small fish could be seen as
they twisted and turned in moments so synchronized it was
as if to a conductor's baton; to their right, the level, fertile
land quickly narrowed and then ended as mountainside
plunged down into the sea; to their left, the fertile land
broadened until it was several hundred metres wide before
it too ended abruptly.

An old man, face lined and wrinkled by time, came out
of the darkness of the interior of the taverna and put two
tall glasses on the table in front of them. Tzoumakas said
something which caused him to nod his head before he went
over to the only other occupied table to take the orders of
three men and one woman.

Tzoumakas drank. 'You will wish to know all. It is little.'
He picked out from one small earthenware dish and ate a
small, square biscuit sprinkled with poppy seeds, then from
another dish a couple of black olives. 'The body goes by
ferry to Palaminoa and the police doctor ring me.' He
dropped the olive stones into the ashtray. 'The Englishman
has a very large blow to the left side of head and skull is
bust, also, inside there is something called . . .' He brought
a piece of paper out of the back pocket of his trousers and
read what was written on it. 'Shall I call it twisting?'

'What happens when the brain moves around the skull
because of the momentum of the blow?'

'Just so. There is membrane tears, bleeding, and so on.
No doubts, the blow kills him. So I ask the doctor, does

the boom of the yacht do this damage? He say, maybe. I ask for better answer. He says, a blow from something solid and wide diameter do much same; doctors never definite in case they is wrong. He also says, Englishman maybe dyes hair grey. I know English is odd, but would a man do that? Of course not. So if I is ill, I will have another doctor who does not talk nonsense.'

'You'll have examined the boom of the yacht?'

'I do this when I secure cabin with padlock. There is nothing. Perhaps there is blood or hair and wind and water take; perhaps there is nothing to take.'

'Does it fit the facts that he was at the wheel when the boom swung across and hit his head?'

'I have his height. I put the height to wheel. If he stands tall and boom comes across – bam! – he can be hit. But who stands tall and not looking when there is perhaps a wind so quick there is only time to notice the sea ripples before it strikes?' He shook his head.

'So what do you think happened?'

'On land there is fools, at sea, many more. But again and again, she says he is sailing for many years, he is good.' He raised his glass and drank. 'To kill, must be reason. If she loves him as she says, there is no reason.'

'But there was a fierce row the previous night?'

'Of course.'

'Has she explained this?'

'She says he is with whore.'

'How's that?'

'A foreign woman owns the east end of the island and is rich to buy all the Dodecanese if for sale. She likes men. She meets men who sail here and takes them to her home. That frightens our wives who say one day she so hungry, she looks at one of us to go home with her.'

'But that hasn't happened yet?'

'The wives say, a husband visits her, he loses much. Yet I think, something frightens, it attracts. One day, some fool husband thinks wife not looking and visits the whore. But a wife is always looking. When he returns, she has knife like razor and before he can lie, he is much less of a man . . . Let us drink more and forget painful things.' Tzoumakas called and the elderly waiter reluctantly shuffled out into the sunshine, took the order, returned indoors.

'Had Señor Perry been with this woman?'

'When yacht arrives Edissovas, they go ashore to taverna and whore is there. They meet. The next day, he says to wife, he wishes a walk, but she stay on yacht because wind may come. Wind is not expected. He is away so long, it is dark. She fears accident, then remembers the whore and how her husband looks at whore in taverna. When he is back, she says he is in whore's bed, doing what whores do so well. He say he walk up mountain and could not come back same way, is difficult to find another route. She says he is one goddamn big liar. They row very hard. Later, row is over and she believes he is true. Is crazy to say she kill man she loves.'

'What do you think happened?'

'When man enjoys all whore gives, it is written on his face and that is what a wife reads.'

'So one really needs to know first of all whether Perry did, or didn't, visit this woman, because that may determine whether Iris Perry eventually believed her husband, the row really was over, and next day all was peace.'

'Indeed.'

'So you've spoken to the woman to find out?'

'You think my wife believes that is why I am at her home? Am I tired of being a man?'

The waiter returned and put down filled glasses, picked up the empty ones. One of the men at the other table called out in French and the waiter shuffled his way across.

'I'd like to talk to her before I have a word with Señora Perry,' Alvarez said. 'Would there be any objection to that?'

'How would wife learn about it?'

'I am not married.'

'Then why should you worry?'

Twenty-Four

Tzoumakas had claimed that the Renault Clio drove better than its appearance might suggest – a very optimistic opinion, Alvarez decided as he coaxed it up to the crest of the narrow road that hugged the side of the mountain. He reached the top and experienced a rush of panic because the road turned sharply left, leaving unfenced space ahead. He braked, even though the car was already moving slowly, and hugged the left-hand side of the road, ignoring the slight possibility of meeting an oncoming car. The road cut through a narrow pass and now with rock to his right he could momentarily relax. Had he known the nature of the drive, he would never have undertaken it.

There was another left-hand corner and then, below him, was the very large house which belonged to the woman the locals called The Whore. Sited on a wedge of rock that stuck out into the sea, it possessed many roof lines, an overhang, a sloping glass face, an awkwardly shaped courtyard, and a square tower. Either many architects had, without reference to each other, planned it or one architect who was convinced harmony could only be found in disharmony.

As the road dipped down, it drew away from the house. When it reached relatively level land, it doubled back and passed through a small packet of arable land to end at the circular drive in front of the house. He climbed out of the car. The nearest edge of rock was several metres to his left, a sufficient distance for him to be able to admire the drama of the setting.

He crossed to the portico, which was fashioned as if for a temple, rang the bell. The heavy, panelled wooden door was opened by a middle-aged, rather ugly woman wearing a maid's apron over a colourful dress. She said something in Greek, he replied in English, she said in very fractured English to enter.

The hall was as large as the whole ground floor of his home in Llueso; the furnishings spoke of wealth unlimited; the huge, beautifully carved marble surround of the large open fireplace held the patina of age and surely had come from some ancient mansion.

He followed the maid along a corridor lined with heavily framed paintings and into a room, bigger than the hall, one side of which was all glass and through which only sea was visible. The maid spoke in Greek. Nadia Gotsev switched off the television. 'You speak English?'

'Yes, I do. I apologize for disturbing you.'

'You relieve the boredom. Come and sit down.'

He sat. Because of what he'd been told by Tzoumakas, he'd expected – a man's mind could scale a dozen absurdities without running out of breath – to meet someone possessed of startling beauty dressed in suggestive clothing, or whose over-ripe features betrayed her wanton nature. She was not beautiful, but high, prominent cheekbones, wide apart, very dark brown eyes, a retroussé nose, curved mouth, and flawless complexion formed a face that was not easily forgotten; her modest dress bore the stamp of expensive simplicity.

'Shall I break the silence?' she said.

'I'm sorry, I was admiring the view.'

'Of the sea?'

A simple question, yet he found himself wondering if . . .

He silently swore. When a man's mind wandered, it was to purple patches. 'It's very dramatic. One could almost be at sea.'

'In winter, when there's a gale, I look out at the rolling waves, the spray lashes the glass, and I'm excited. Quick movement always excites me.'

So when she . . . 'It must be very dramatic,' he said hurriedly, before realizing he was repeating himself.

'Can I offer you something to drink?'

'Thank you, señora . . . señorita . . .'

She smiled. 'Call me Nadia and avoid any uncertainty. Will you join me in some Krug?'

'Would you mind if I had coñac with ice?'

'Why should I mind? Isn't the freedom to enjoy what one desires the road to happiness?'

'I suppose so,' he mumbled, hoping she'd no idea what his mind was desiring.

She turned and spoke to the maid, who left. 'You haven't told me your first name,' she said, as the maid closed the door behind herself.

'Enrique.'

'You are Spanish?'

'Mallorquin.'

'There is a large difference?'

'A very large one.'

'You speak with much heart! Are you a man of passion?'

To keep his mind off the question she had just asked, he extolled the beauty of the island and in particular of Llueso Bay.

'You live on Mount Olympus! So tell me, what do you do when you're not drinking nectar and eating ambrosia?'

'I am a member of the Cuerpo General de Policia.'

'A policeman? But you look so unaggressive! Is that a cloak?'

She was laughing at him. 'I'll leave you to decide.'

'That may take time. Perhaps you wear many cloaks?' After a moment, she said: 'You are obviously a man who likes to think before he speaks.'

'My seniors would deny that possibility.'

'Seniors deny everything to prove they are seniors.'

The door opened and the maid returned with a tray. She crossed to a beautifully inlaid rosewood occasional table, put the tray down, picked the bottle of champagne out of the ice bucket and filled a glass, handed the glass to Nadia; she poured cognac into a large balloon glass, looked at Alvarez, spoke.

'She wants to know if you really want some ice?'

He hesitated.

'It's unusual, Enrique, but what is more exciting than the unusual?'

Was she referring only to ice in cognac? 'Three cubes, please.'

She spoke to the maid who, using silver tongs, picked up ice from the insulated container and dropped it into the glass. She handed him the glass, left.

'What do we drink to?' Nadia asked.

'Whatever you suggest.'

'How very careful of you,' she said mockingly. 'We will drink to the future. May it bring us what we would wish.'

Had she an idea of where his wishes were straying? . . . 'The future,' he mumbled, then drank. It was cognac of the finest quality; no wonder the maid had queried the ice.

'I know your name, Enrique, that you are a careful man, you love your home, and you are a quiet policeman, but you haven't yet explained why you've come here to see me.'

He was grateful for the chance to clear his mind of extraneous matters. 'The Cuerpo was asked by the local police if we could help them in their investigations concerning . . . You have heard of the death of Señor Perry?'

'This is a small island where the bush telegraph is faster than the telephone, which so often doesn't work.'

Clearly, his death had not affected her. 'Since it seemed possible I might be able to assist, I flew to Rhodes and then came on by ferry. I met Señor Tzoumakas and he told me the facts.'

'As a consequence of which, you came here?'

'Yes.'

'You think I can say what happened when Basil died aboard his yacht?'

'No, of course not.'

'Then why should you think I might be able to tell you anything of the slightest consequence? Perhaps . . .'

There was a silence, which he ended. 'Perhaps what?'

'Perhaps it was more my reputation that drew you here?'

'Your reputation?' he repeated, trying to sound perplexed.

'You have not been told what that is?'

'No.'

'You are a liar.' She drank. 'I like liars because they always have character, whether good or bad. Honest men are so very dreary . . . So now you can tell me whether I am the woman you expected to meet?'

'I'd no preconceptions . . .' He noted her sarcastic smile. 'All right, no, you're not.'

'Good. I'd hate to discover I can be predicted. Does the reality gladden or depress you?'

'If I knew what the reality was, I could answer.'

'Surely in your job you should be able to judge?'

'Women have always mystified me.'

'Who could deny a man brave enough to admit that?'

Deny him what? 'Do you mind if now I ask you a few questions?'

231

'So long as they're personal.'

'Is it right you met the Perrys in a taverna?'

'Of course.'

'How did it happen?'

'How does it always happen? The two of them arrived, Basil saw me and in no time found an excuse to start talking to me.'

'Did that worry his wife?'

'Small-minded wives always dislike their husbands talking to other women.'

'She was annoyed?'

She shrugged her shoulders.

'Presumably, you don't know the details of Perry's death?'

'I'm not interested in them. The exotic intrigues, the sordid bores.'

'When the yacht returned, he was unconscious and he did not regain consciousness before he was pronounced dead. According to his wife, she was below in the cabin when the yacht was caught in a wind squall and the boom swept across to crash into his head.'

'But she is not believed?'

'There are some inconsistencies in what she says. Moreover, the previous night when the yacht was at anchor, a couple in another yacht heard them having a very bitter row.'

'What would one expect since they were married?'

'Some marriages are happy.'

'None of mine was. Are you married?'

'No.'

'Surely your pleasures don't lie in other directions?'

'No.'

'I thought not.'

'My novia died many years ago.'

232

'And you have remained faithful to her memory?'

'Yes.'

'Why?'

'That's my business.'

'You're leaving me to guess?'

'According to Señora Perry, the row was a consequence of her husband's having spent much of the afternoon and evening with you. Did he, in fact, come here and visit you?'

'What a polite way of expressing his hopeful intentions!'

'Did he?'

'That doesn't matter.'

'I assure you, it does.'

'I never accept a man's assurance for fear I'll believe him.'

'It could be important.'

'Not to me.'

'To the investigation.'

'Because you're suggesting she hit him with something very solid?'

'I'm not suggesting anything.'

'Nothing? Surely you don't want to be that boring?'

'Did he come here?'

'She's far too weak to have killed him.'

'The row was described as sounding very bitter.'

'The weaker the woman, the more bitterly she rows.'

'Why do you keep calling her weak?'

'She saw her husband ogling me, but was ready to forgive him even while he was trying to make me think he was God's gift to women.'

'How could you judge that?'

'She was so infatuated with him, she'd have forgiven him a sultan's harem. Quite nauseating since she was married to him.'

'You could infer all that from one brief meeting at the taverna?'

'Of course.'

'Your judgment could be hopelessly wrong.'

'It never is.'

'Then how come you've been married more than once?'

She laughed. 'When you entered here, you tried to be a nobody; so unassuming, so polite. But I could judge you liked to wear a mouse's coat because then people underestimate you . . . You're curious about the men I married, aren't you?'

'No.'

'Then I will tell you. They tried to wear lions' coats. Each of the three liked my money much more than me, but couldn't quite conceal that fact; each thought he was so irresistible, it was an honour to be courted by him. So I kept my money to myself and made each one of them realize he was very resistible.'

'You obviously initially misread the character of each one.'

'On the contrary.'

'Why marry if you knew?'

'To enjoy the pleasure of deflating them.'

'That sounds like nonsense.'

'Only to a pedestrian mind.' She drained her glass, held it up. 'You can refill this.'

'When you say please.'

She smiled. 'There's more man in you than my three husbands put together! They used to think that the more they jumped, the more I'd be taken in by them . . . Dear Enrique, please pour me another drink.'

He stood, crossed to the occasional table, picked up the bottle out of the ice bucket, refilled her glass. As he refilled his own and added three ice cubes, she said: 'Don't you think my husbands deserved the treatment they received?'

As he handed her her glass, he said: 'If there's even a thread of truth in what you're telling me, there's a cruel streak in you.' He returned to his chair.

'If pleasure's to be enjoyed to the full, it needs to be touched with cruelty.'

'More nonsense.'

'You believe love is pure?'

'It can be.'

'A romantic! You become fascinatingly more complicated by the moment.'

The door opened and the maid stepped just inside the room and spoke rapidly. Nadia answered her and she left.

'She asked if you liked lobster. I assured her that you might put ice into cognac, but you undoubtedly enjoyed all pleasures in your own personal style.'

'Why did she ask?'

'To know if she should serve lobster for dinner.'

'I'll be leaving here as soon as I have your answer.'

'To what question?'

'Was Señor Perry here that afternoon and evening?'

'Can't you think of something much more interesting to ask me?'

Of course he could. And he was convinced she knew what that something was. But how would she react to his asking it? . . . Sweet Mary! What was in his glass apart from superb cognac and ice – oysters, red hot peppers?

As they left the dining-room and went through to the sitting-room, he looked at his watch.

'You are an impatient man?' she asked.

'It's getting late and I don't know if the hotel has a night porter.' He remained standing as she sat on one of the two settees.

'How is that important?'

'I don't want to be locked out.'

'So you are intending to leave very soon?'

'When you've told me whether Señor Perry came here.'

'My lips are sealed. If you can't find the magic to open them, return to your flea-ridden hotel. Otherwise, come and sit by my side.'

He tried to argue with himself, but that merely showed what a fool he could be. He crossed the room and settled by her side.

He stared up at the ceiling. Occasionally, very occasionally, reality outstripped a man's imagination . . . She moved to rest her breasts on his chest. 'You're older, but you're more of a man!' She reached across with her right hand and gripped him so hard, he yelped. 'There's the pain; now, the pleasure will be even greater,' she mumured, just before her mouth closed on his.

She stirred sugar into her coffee. 'My heart is very sad.'

About to eat another mouthful of the croissant-shaped pastry whose taste resembled an ensaimada, he lowered his hand, said: 'Why's that?'

'In two hours, the helicopter arrives to take me to Athens.'

'But . . . but why?'

'I should hate to hurt you, Enrique. I think perhaps you are a good man.'

'Why should you hurt me by staying here?'

'Because I am the woman I am. Many of us are driven by devils and mine are too strong for me to control them.'

He ate. Did her worst devil always convince her she no longer wanted what she had just attained? He tried to call on logic to ease his sense of impending loss. She was an immensely wealthy, worldly woman, he was a devalued inspector of peasant stock; she would be at ease in sophisticated surroundings, he would not; for her, a close relationship was to be gained and then broken, for him, it was to be enjoyed ever more deeply. They were totally dissimilar characters who had known each other only for hours . . . Yet acknowledging all that, there was much pain in knowing he would never see her again.

The threshing of the helicopter rotor made speech difficult. As the maid, ducking lower than necessary, went to the cabin to hand two suitcases to a crew member, Nadia kissed Alvarez with passion. She stepped back, opened her Gucci handbag and brought out a small case wrapped in green tissue paper. 'To remind you of me.'

'I won't need anything to do that.'

'Time kills memories, mementoes keep them alive.' She kissed him again, turned, took a pace towards the helicopter.

'You've never answered the question,' he shouted.

She turned back. 'If you are as sharp as I know you to be despite that mouse's coat, you'll find the answer for yourself.' She looked at him, her eyes searching his face, her expression sad, then turned back and hurried into the helicopter. The crew member followed her, raised the steps, shut the door. The rotor turned more fiercely and the helicopter rose. She waved once, then was no longer visible through the porthole.

He walked over to the battered Clio and settled behind the wheel. He brought the package out of his pocket and unwrapped it. A gold cigarette case, the lid of which was engraved with what looked like five stars set in the form of a sideways W and under which was the single word 'Cassiopeia'. He put the case down on the passenger seat.

The engine started at the fourth attempt. His mind was so filled with memories that on the drive back he forgot to be frightened by the precipitous drops which bordered the narrow, twisting road.

Twenty-Five

Alvarez crossed to the table set outside the taverna at which Tzoumakas sat. 'Sorry I'm late.'

'You look tired. Were I a wife, should I read much into that?'

'Not if you were a loyal wife,' he answered as he settled on the uncomfortable metal chair.

'Is there one that loyal?'

The old man came out from the taverna, took Alvarez's order, returned inside.

'Did she give you what you wish? I say quick, I mean the answer to the question.' Tzoumakas smiled.

'She refused to tell me, however much I pressed her.'

'Perhaps you begin to hurt?'

'I think you have a nasty mind.'

'I believe so. Now I tell you what happen. The wife will be in hotel in Edissovas. Since it is but ten minutes to drive, we do not rush.'

'Has she said anything more?'

'Again and again, she loves her husband. She cannot hurt him. She speaks so strong, I almost believe.'

'When they were in Mallorca, I had every reason to judge she loved him very much. Also, Señora Gotsev reckons she did.'

'Then . . .' Tzoumakas shrugged his shoulders.

Alvarez stared out to sea. A large yacht was now at

anchor and a man was washing down the deck. A paid crew member? When one saw so much wealth, one dismally wondered why it passed one by.

The waiter brought them two cups of aromatic, very strong coffee and a jug of milk. Alvarez spooned sugar into his cup, added milk. He produced his new cigarette case, which he'd filled, and offered it. After Tzoumakas had taken a cigarette, he helped himself to one, closed the case and put it down on the table while he reached into his pocket for matches.

Tzoumakas studied the case, which was lid side up. 'There is many coin . . . What you say?'

'Coincidences?'

'Just so.'

'What makes you say that?'

'Your cigarette case.'

'How is that a coincidence?'

'I will tell. Yesterday night, I go aboard yacht to search from stem to stern to find something that help; I find nothing. Life always is difficult . . . In a drawer, under clothes, is cigarette case like yours, but different. The stars is the Southern Cross. But case is for sure made by same people. I say, this coincidence.'

'Not really.'

'But it is!'

'It's merely one person giving similar presents to two people.' He spoke with sharp bitterness. He believed she had given him a special keepsake because even in the short time they had been together, he had come to mean as much to her as she to him; why did men have such a capacity to delude themselves over women? Was it because they did that she gained a perverse pleasure from knowing each dismissed lover would fool himself . . . 'We can be certain Señor Perry spent time with Señora Gotsev.'

'But why?'

'Because.'

'I hear!' Tzoumakas smiled. 'But I no understand . . . Now again, the row of great importance and the whore . . . Perhaps I must not call her that to you; perhaps her words are nothing.'

'I can't forget how Señor and Señora Perry used to look at each other.'

They were silent for a while, then Tzoumakas suggested that another cup of coffee would be welcome; doubly welcome if accompanied by a glass of brandy – and not the local stuff which a man drank only because he was thirsty, but the brandy that was imported from Spain. What better way to cement a friendship than to drink Spanish brandy?

Half an hour later, Tzoumakas said: 'I go for car and drive Edissovas.' He stood. 'If only she say husband a poor sailor, how much more easy for us. But she say, he very good one. Yet he stands proud and does not see a wind . . .' He shook his head.

'She'd probably claim he was a very poor helmsman if all the evidence didn't suggest he was a very good and experienced one.'

'Is so. Things never as one wishes.' He began to walk.

Alvarez looked down at the cigarette case on the table by the side of his coffee cup and saucer. The sun was reflecting off it and sending a circle of brightness up on to the underside of the sun umbrella that protected the table. Was each man given a different design or did she just bring one out of wherever she kept the many, careless what constellation of stars was engraved and named? Yet something – stupid hope? – nagged his mind and said that there was significance to the gift. But she couldn't know when he'd been born; in any case, he was fairly certain Cassiopeia was not one of the twelve signs of the zodiac. And certainly the Southern

241

Cross wasn't. Could there then be – hope on hope – some hidden message in the stars? . . . A sudden thought exploded in his mind. 'Evangelos,' he called out.

Tzoumakas came to a halt.

'Do you know how many stars there are in the Southern Cross?'

'Four.'

And there were five in Cassiopeia. Hadn't she told him he was a great lover for an older man? She had given him room for pride . . . An older man. My God! he silently shouted, I have been blind, deaf, and dumb.

They sat in the small bedroom – Iris Perry in one chair, Alvarez and Tzoumakas in the two others which the staff had brought them.

'Why won't you understand?' she said wildly, speaking directly to Alvarez. 'You saw us together in Majorca. Surely to God you realized I loved him so much that I'd have hurt myself rather than him?'

'That is certainly what I judged.'

'Then how can you begin to think I murdered him? It was an accident, a ghastly, terrible, stupid accident.'

'Your husband was a very experienced yachtsman, was he not?'

'Yes, but . . . Anyone can make a mistake.'

'Would not a very experienced yachtsman have been keeping the keenest possible watch for a sudden wind squall, knowing that they frequently happened off this island? Would he have been standing tall so that if somehow he was caught unawares by a squall, the beam would sweep across and catch him?'

'He must have been thinking of something so hard he forgot the danger.' Her lips trembled and tears spilled down her cheeks.

'Why did your husband dye his moustache and hair grey?'

She brushed the tears from her cheeks. Suddenly, her face expressed fright as well as grief.

'One meets many men who wish to look younger, but very few who try to look older.'

'I don't know what you're talking about.'

'When I first arrived at Ca'n Isault and you opened the door and I said I was a detective, you were shocked. At the time, I thought this was because the English are so law-abiding that they have only to meet a policeman to remember when they parked on a solid blue line. But that wasn't why you were upset, was it?'

'What are you getting at?'

Tzoumakas looked curiously at Alvarez.

'Later, you told me an unknown Englishman had called relatively recently, but your husband insisted it was quite some time before; Matilde agreed with you. You mentioned him as an insurance, didn't you?'

'Insurance against what?'

'My learning – probably from Matilde – that you had had a visitor. You should have consulted with your husband before saying anything.'

'This is ridiculous.'

'That time you returned home and found me talking to Matilde in your sitting-room, you were shocked to see me; but still more shocked when you heard the name Gates. What does all this add up to?'

She gave no answer.

'Again, when I was speaking to Rivera, an assistant harbour-master in Port Llueso, your yacht sailed in – or perhaps out, I can't remember – and he remarked that you handled her much better than did your husband who could be rather granny-knot. Yet you had done no yachting before your marriage, whilst your husband had over many years.'

She sat in a strained position, as if all her muscles were tensed.

'Señor Pearson, at Steadfast Security, was talking to me and remarked that Señor Perry lacked a sense of humour. Yet I remembered him as having a very obvious sense of humour. Except, that is, when he was furious because you told me Matilde had spoken to Señor Gates – which meant he had called at your house.'

'Why are you saying all this? What's it matter?'

'It matters a great deal. These various, unrelated facts prove you did not kill your husband here, on your yacht.'

For several seconds, it seemed his words had no meaning for her. Then she cried, her voice high and thin: 'You know I didn't kill him?'

'Yes.'

'Oh, my God! It's been a ghastly nightmare . . .' She faced Tzoumakas. 'Did you hear?' she shouted. 'I didn't kill him. He knows I didn't. It doesn't matter what you think, I didn't kill him.'

Tzoumakas's expression betrayed his perplexity, but he still did not speak.

'The man who died by accident on the *Argo* was not your husband,' Alvarez said.

The change from elation to fear was so swift that she might have received a violent blow in the stomach.

'He was Ivor Keen, a man who was many things, but no queer as you told your husband.'

'No,' she shouted.

'Your husband was older than you, far from exciting, but rich. Keen was younger than you, very exciting, and poor. A man with a missing conscience but all the charm in the world, he set out to make you fall headlong in love with him, possibly to enjoy the pleasure of planting horns on a man he hated solely because of wealth, certainly with

244

the idea of eventually enriching himself. You weren't as adept at deception as he'd hoped and it became clear that somehow you'd been sufficiently injudicious to arouse your husband's suspicions, so Keen told you that if you didn't do as he suggested, either your relationship with him would have to end or your husband would gain proof of your infidelity and, possessing a vindictive character, would throw you out with as little of his money as he could manage. The prospect of losing the security and luxury you'd known since marriage frightened you; but at first, his plan terrified you even more. But then, as happens when desire faces conscience, you began to wonder; to wonder is the first step, but the largest, to agreeing.

'Keen was very smart. He had read your husband's character and was certain he would try to entrap you if he couldn't get the evidence any other way. And so when he said he wanted to go for a solo sail, Keen recognized the bait for what it was. When your husband sailed off on his own, he stayed away from you when circumstances must suggest that if he really were your lover, he'd seize the opportunity to be with you. When your husband got in touch with Steadfast Security fairly early on, they reported that so far there'd been no contact. Then, later, you got in touch with him on the yacht and told him how much you were missing him and how you wanted to join him on a long cruise which would let the two of you regain the magic of early days. He said to meet him at Biarritz.

'You boarded the yacht there; so, a little later, did Keen. Your husband was murdered and when at sea, his weighted body was thrown over the side.

'You and Keen, now apparently your husband, with forged documents to back up his new identity, arrived at Port Llueso and rented a house well away from the tourist areas because then there was still less chance of meeting someone who had known your husband. Whilst there, Keen – through forgery and with your help – set about transferring all your husband's assets into accounts to which you both had access. I don't suppose it occurred to you that once he was in a position to put his hands on everything, your life was at risk.'

'No!' she cried.

'Things were proceeding very smoothly until Gates arrived, ostensibly to present the firm's final report, in fact to point out that their account had not been paid. It's strange how life so often moves to tiny insignificances. Had that bill been settled earlier, Gates would not have called at Ca'n Isault and he would not have been killed because he could identify Basil Perry. Had the husband of my cousin's cousin not been suspected of smuggling . . . A different story, but it became part of this one. Had Keen been able to resist Nadia's charms, he would not have spent time with her; you would not have accused him of betraying you, there would have been no row, there would have been little or no suspicion. Had he been anything of a yachtsman, he would not have stood tall – as they say here – and ignored the signs of an approaching wind squall; had you not been preparing a meal, you would have been on deck and there would have been no such stupidity. Had I not been given a cigarette case . . .' He became silent.

'It's all ridiculous,' she said hoarsely.

'You are faced with difficult choices. Do you admit Keen was not your husband? Do you admit what happened to Basil Perry? Do you admit your lover murdered your husband in Biarritz and you were at the very least an accessory to that murder, perhaps as well to Gates's, so that you can say, and be believed, that Keen was accidently killed on the yacht because he was no seaman; or do you deny that it was Keen who was on the yacht and face the charge of murdering your husband? You will have to think very carefully before you decide.'

Not too long now before he could wander off to Club Llueso for his merienda . . . The phone rang.

'It's Perfect Car Hire here,' a woman said. 'I'm calling with reference to the notice sent round by you some time ago asking for certain information. I'm afraid the notice somehow got put on one side . . . I hope you can understand?'

'Of course.' One should be generous.

'We had a booking that began at the end of May which was for just short of a month and the car, a white Renault Mégane, has still not been returned to any of our garages.'

'Presumably if it's overdue for . . .' – he looked at the small calendar which Fuster had kept on the side of the desk and he hadn't yet thrown away since it depicted a scene in Barcelona – '. . . for roughly a month and a half, you've reported it to Traffic as missing?'

'No.'

'How's that?'

'When this sort of thing happens, we assume the hirer has stayed on the island for longer than intended and since the original payment was by credit card, we merely advise the card company of the added debit or debits.'

A useful way of making certain someone else was the loser. 'What was the name of the hirer?'

'The one mentioned in your notice – Gates. D'you think he's taken the car off the island to sell with false papers?'

'No. He's dead. It will be parked somewhere. You'd better tell Traffic to start looking for it.'

'Can you do that?'

'I'm afraid the request has to come from the informant. Suggest they start in Port Llueso since that is probably where it was driven to. If they find it, let me know.' He thanked her for the call, replaced the receiver. Almost immediately, the phone rang again. It was to be hoped this would not be a long call or his merienda would be badly interrupted.

'The superior chief wishes to speak to you,' said the plum-voiced secretary.

He waited.

Since they'd last spoken, Salas's attitude had once more changed. There was no good morning, no expressed wish that all was well. 'I have received a call from the Greek police. Señora Perry has made a statement in which she claims she had no idea Keen intended to murder her husband and was utterly shocked when this happened. Keen then frightened her into silence. Equally, she had no idea he intended to kill Gates, has no idea when and where this took place and only became aware of the murder when she was told about it. The death of Keen was pure accident.'

'I suppose she will get away with being an accessory rather than a principal in her husband's case.'

'And in the murder of Gates?'

'That was so brutally carried out that I think one can accept her statement.'

'She might well have offered a false friendship to lure him.'

'You're suggesting that recognizing he was a randy character, she showed a lot of leg as a come-on?'

'How dare you suggest I would make such a disgusting suggestion.'

'My apologies, señor.'

'You are content to rest all the blame on Keen's shoulders?'

'If one does accept her statement, then as far as we are concerned, with Keen dead, the case can be closed. And since Señor Perry was murdered in Biarritz, and Keen died in Greece, we have no jurisdiction, and therefore no part to play, in further proceedings.'

'She is to escape both judgment and punishment?'

'She will be judged, and probably punished, because of her husband's death.'

'Hardly an ethical or legal response to the facts.'

'I was thinking along practical lines. But if you deem it necessary to investigate the question of the degree of her involvement in Gates's murder which, of course, means in effect challenging her admission that Keen alone was guilty of it, this will be a long and very difficult task because the truth is, there is very little, if any, hard evidence against her and precious little more against Keen. We might spend weeks, even months, getting nowhere.'

'I will give the matter thought.'

'Very well, señor. There is something more that concerns me. Has Emilio Perello been released?'

'Yes.'

'The poor chap must have become very confused and distraught?'

'Possibly.'

'I'm sure you'll agree that it would be a good idea if I apologize to his mother for Inspector Fuster's mistakes?'

'If you wish.'

'By the way, I haven't heard if the amalgamation is still to go ahead despite all that's happened? The thing is, if it is, you will be putting the proposal to the director general for his approval on the grounds of increased efficiency and in these circumstances I'm sure I'd feel entitled to submit a respectful suggestion that the idea be vetoed and to give my reason for that. This would raise a problem. My submission would naturally have to record the fact that from the beginning I held Perello could not have been guilty of the murder because of the evidence, but Inspector Fuster declined to listen to me. And according to him – naturally, I am confident that this is, at best, an exaggeration, at worst, a lie – you supported his opinion . . . .'

'I have decided not to propose an amalgamation.'

'I have to confess I am glad of that.'

'And I—' Salas began, then slammed down the receiver before he could make his confession.